PARTIALLY BROKEN NEVER DESTROYED
MIRROR MIRROR

Nataisha T. Hill

Copyright Nataisha T Hill 2013

Chapter 1

It was a beautiful spring Saturday in the middle of April and the soft breeze gave the evening calmness as footprints set across the sky. Kayla was sitting on the porch of the three-bedroom house she was renting about ten minutes away from her mom's home. She decided to move back to her hometown in order for her and her son Nicholas, who was now four, to be closer to her family. She had gotten a job at the Fairview Medical Hospital as a licensed practical nurse. In the fall, she was planning to enroll in the graduate nursing program to become a registered nurse and perhaps even pursue her PhD. Things seemed to be looking up for her financially and career wise, but Kayla was having an entirely different experience with her personal life.

Kayla found herself feeling frustrated. She could not believe she had gotten involved in another relationship after promising herself she would slow down. It was already close to five in the evening and she had spent the day arguing. It was Kayla's first full day she had off in two months and her new boyfriend, Raymond, wanted to hangout with his friends instead of going somewhere with her.

"Raymond, you promised on my next day off that we were going to go somewhere special. My mom is watching Nicholas and I just spent two and a half hours getting ready."

"Kayla, you didn't tell me you were off today until Tuesday. I had already told you that my cousin may be coming down from Chicago this weekend."

"Raymond, the keyword is 'may.' Do you know how long I have been waiting for a day off?"

"Not as long as I've been waiting for my cousin to come down," Raymond argued.

"You told me your cousin is going to be here all week, Raymond. You know I am working crazy hours at the hospital and-"

"Okay," he interrupted, "I'll go and see him for a minute and then take you out."

After hanging up with Raymond, Kayla felt as if she still had lost the argument. Even though he did agree to take her out, she knew he was going to be acting as if it was something she forced him to do. It almost made her want to call back and say forget it, but she knew that would only start another argument.

It was almost 6:30 and Raymond still had not made it over. Kayla attempted to call him twice, but her calls went straight to his voicemail. Every minute that passed seemed like an hour. Although Raymond was a generally nice fellow, he could be very shallow at times and spoiled. Raymond's mom was head of her dentistry facility and his dad was a retired college coach and owned a landscaping company, so they were in the upper-class ranking.

The only children were Raymond and his sister, Erica, so they pretty much had gotten everything they had ever asked for from their parents. Kayla had actually met Raymond at his mom's dentist office when she had gone to get her check-up. He had started making jokes about how long it normally took to get back to see the dentist. Of course, Kayla had always been a sucker for a guy who could make her laugh. What made his jokes even more hysterical was when he finally told her the dentist was his mom. Raymond wasn't the most handsome man she had ever dated, but he was decent looking with hazel eyes and a tall muscular build.

After waiting another hour, Kayla finally decided to take matters into her own hands. It was not as if they had been dating two weeks or so, this was like the fifth month into the relationship. Raymond had done some selfish things in the past, but he had never cut off his phone so that she wouldn't be able to reach him. As she got into the car, all types of thoughts had begun to entertain her mind. She thought that maybe he had been in a car accident or would if something happened to someone in his family.

At that moment, a very different thought came to her mind. What if Raymond's so-called cousin was actually an out-of-town fling?

Raymond lived with his parents, so she couldn't just up and knock on the door whenever she felt like it. The last thing she wanted was to have his mom and dad in their business. Raymond's house was set back a distance from street view and the driveway was long. Kayla knew she couldn't speed by and see if Raymond's car was there, because they lived off a dead-end street.

She decided she would park on the corner of the main road and Raymond's street, then get out and walk. After rounding the corner, she noticed there were about thirty cars parked in the driveway. There wasn't anyone out front; therefore, the celebration must have been inside or out back in their private pool house.

Kayla cut through the patch of perfectly trimmed bushes that lined the driveway. By the time she was near the center of the cars, she noticed a car up front that resembled Raymond's silver mustang. She assumed it had to have been Raymond's car. As she turned around and headed back towards her car, she couldn't help but wonder why Raymond did not invite her to the celebration. She had already met his parents, his aunts, and a few of his cousins, not to mention, both grandparents. Even more, she and Raymond's snobbish sister were now getting along. As thoughts began to entertain her mind again, Kayla found herself interrupted by a familiar voice.

"Hey, Kayla, what are you doing out here and where is Raymond?

Kayla could feel her heart beating a thousand times per minute. She didn't know how to respond to the question. She turned around and faced Mr. Jenson, Raymond's father.

"S...Sir?" she stammered.

"Did Raymond go in the house?" he asked.

"Oh, I'm just getting here," she responded trying to dodge any other direct questions. It appeared that Mr. Jenson had been drinking, so she assumed short answers would be best.

"He would have his woman to walk up here by herself, come around here sweetheart," he said as he motioned her to follow him around back.

"I don't know what I'm going to do with that son of mine," he said as he continued to ramble, "if its not one thing it's another."

At that point, she knew Mr. Jenson had been drinking heavily because she could smell the aroma of cologne and whisky through his skin. As they walked and made small talk towards the back, Kayla noticed that Mr. Jenson continuously reached in his pocket while looking back towards the car. Paying close attention to his awkwardness, she began to wonder the reason of him hanging out by the cars alone. He had to have been out there for a while because she did not see anyone coming out from the back when she first peeked around the corner. As they opened the door to the fenced-in backyard, Mr. Jenson looked at Kayla with an unsettling expression.

"You know," he started, "people usually reveal themselves way before they ever look in the mirror."

Kayla did not know who he was referring to or what to expect.

Kayla followed Mr. Jenson over to the section where there were familiar faces. She noticed Erica on the opposite side talking to a group of females. She cut her eyes and waved at Kayla while continuing to chat with the others.

"Hey, everybody, look who I found!" Mr. Jenson contentedly yelled, walking her into the crowd. It was very strange how he just changed his demeanor within twenty seconds.

"Hello Kayla," Mrs. Jenson smiled as she walked forward to give her a hug. Mrs. Jenson was wearing a tan khaki dress that complemented her short, medium build and highlighted hair. Even though she was turning forty- four, she still looked as stunning as if she was in her early thirties and she always kept up with the latest trends. She was totally opposite of Mr. Jenson who was tall, plain looking, and for the most part, wore Dickies and Polo shirts daily.

"Raymond said he was on his way to get you, but I understand, he procrastinates like his father," she joked.

"I reckon," Kayla said apprehensively. She glanced over at Mr. Jenson who did not seem amused by his wife's comment.

"Well, Kayla, you know when you're here, you're home, so treat yourself to the food in the kitchen and drinks are over by the bar."

Once Mrs. Jenson smiled and walked off, Kayla sat down while noticing Mr. Jenson staring intensely at his wife.

He was acting particularly strange and making her feel uncomfortable. He finally got up and disappeared toward the front. She finally looked down at her phone and saw that Raymond had not called. How was Raymond on his way to pick her up when he hadn't even called to tell her he was on his way?

About thirty minutes went by and there was still no sign of Raymond. Kayla continued to mingle with a few of Raymond's cousins while having a few cocktails. Just as she was finishing her fourth drink, Erica walked her way with a handsome gentleman by her side.

"Hey, Kayla, are you enjoying the party?" Erica asked.

"Yeah, I think it's nice. It is always good to be around good people and good food," Kayla responded.

"Excuse my manners, Kayla; this is my good friend Bryan."

"Hello, Kayla, how are you?" Bryan asked as he reached out his hand to finalize the introduction.

"I'm good, can't complain," Kayla responded smiling as she embraced his gesture. He was even more handsome up close. He had a brown paper-bag skin tone, a low haircut with waves that would make anyone sea sick, and his smile had Kayla secretly melting.

"I could get you another drink if you would like me to," he offered.

"That sounds good." She started to wonder, is this man trying to flirt on the sly or is he just being nice.

"Girl, you are going to be toasted by the time my brother gets here, speaking of which, where is he anyway?"

"You know how your brother is sometimes." Kayla decided to keep her answer vague. She couldn't determine if she was sensing a little hostility from Erica since her guy had offered to get Kayla a drink or if she was trying to go somewhere else with that question.

"So, where is your son?"

"Why? Do you want to keep him?" Kayla knew that Erica was trying to start something, because she had never asked about Nicholas before. As matter of fact, when Kayla and Raymond first started dating, she told Raymond he should not hook up with a woman who had a child.

"What? I can't ask about my soon to be nephew?" she giggled.

"I think you need to stop while you're ahead," Kayla sternly stated.

"Ladies, let's depart," Bryan intervened while escorting Erica away, "and I still got that drink coming up for you, Kayla."

Had this tramp lost her mind Kayla wondered? The old her would have went clean off on her ass. She thought she and Erica had reconciled, but it seemed as if every time Kayla would get to know someone Erica cared about, Erica would get insecure. Erica was cute with a nice figure, college student, no kids, and even had her own little crib, so Kayla could not understand where the jealousy was coming from.

About fifteen minutes had passed by, so Kayla was about to get up and get her own drink.

Before she could, Bryan came around the corner with two drinks in his hands. Raymond was lucky that she was really into him because Bryan was almost irresistible.

"Just as I promised, Ms. Kayla," he said smiling.

"I really do appreciate it and I'm sorry you had to see the serious side of me after only three minutes of meeting me," she joked.

"It's all good. I like people that are themselves around anyone. It kind of eliminates false images that people sometime portray. So, I take it you're Raymond's girl, right?"

"Yeah, we've been trying to push it through," she sighed as she took a gulp of the martini that was in her hand.

"It hasn't been that hard has it?" he asked as he was laughing at Kayla's gesture.

"Not really, but...I don't know. These days you never know what to expect." The fact that he was Erica's friend and she did not know this guy very well made her resist the temptation to open up to him.

"Well," he said discretely pointing to the phone that was in her hand, "if you ever want to talk you can call me at this number, 555-7171."

After giving her his number, he instantly got up and left from the sitting area. Kayla wasn't sure if she should put his number in her phone.

She thought that maybe it could have been a scheme that Erica created in order to break up her and Raymond. Besides, she figured it would be an easy number to remember if she did decide to call it.

Kayla had now been at the party over an hour and still no sign of Raymond. She took her final sip as she got ready to get up and head towards Raymond's mom to tell her goodnight. Just as she was picking up her purse, Bryan came over.

"I know you're not leaving this early," he joked.

"Yeah, I think it's time for me to call it a night, besides, I'm sure my baby boy misses me."

"How old is your son?"

"He just turned five this year," she responded.

"That's what's up. I can dig that. You're not going to wait on Raymond?" he asked suspiciously.

"No, I guess he'll come by my crib later on if he isn't too drunk or what not."

"Speaking of the devil, there he is right there," Bryan said pointing towards Raymond.

"Where?" she questioned as she attempted to look through the small crowd of people. Kayla turned to follow the direction of where Bryan, who was now looking at her in awe, had pointed; she noticed the room had suddenly grown quiet. She moved passed the crowd toward Raymond only to see him standing there with another woman under his arm.

Chapter 2

Kayla stood face to face with Raymond who was looking like a deer in headlights. She glanced at the small woman who looked as if she could have been Raymond's cute little cousin. Kayla felt déjà vu all over again as tears began to well in her eyes. She could feel the adrenaline rushing through every blood vessel in her body. She was having the exact same out-of-body experience she had when she caught Jeremy. The girl standing under Raymond's arm removed herself from his grasp, dramatically raised her hand in the air, and looked at Raymond. She acted confused about what was going on. All eyes were on Raymond who remained staring into the eyes of Kayla. The toughest knife on earth could not cut the tension in the room.

Kayla stood there tense and unaware of what she may do if Raymond or his friend girl said or did the wrong thing. She was waiting on Raymond to ask or say anything she didn't like. She was even more ready for the female he was with to put her two cents in the matter.

"Can we go somewhere and talk?" Raymond asked in a deep sorrow filled voice.

"Wait a minute, what do you mean can yall go somewhere and talk?" the little female argued.

"I don't have time for this, Melody; I got something I need to handle as a man." Raymond demanded.

"You call this being a man, Raymond?" Kayla heatedly interrupted.

"Hold on, both of you need to back up off my brother," Erica chimed in, walking her way over to the commotion.

The young female seemed slightly startled and embarrassed by Erica's direct approach. She waved her hand and walked away mumbling something about dikes and faggots.

"You're welcome to follow her," Erica mocked as she directed her attention towards Kayla.

Kayla was infuriated and taken to the point of no return. She had alcohol in her system, a cheating boyfriend to deal with, and his crazy ass sister who had been getting on her nerves since day one. Kayla hurriedly walked up to Erica and put her pointer finger on her forehead.

"You got one more time to say anything that I don't like and I'm going to give you what you're asking for," Kayla threaten.

"Hold on," Raymond said as he grabbed Kayla, "this is my fault and I'm the one you should be upset with."

"Get your hands off me," Kayla yelled, jerking away from Raymond. "We have nothing left to say to one another."

"Kayla, please…just let me talk to you in private."

"Why are you even….ugghhh," Erica groaned as she stormed off. She probably knew that was the best move for her.

"Kayla," Raymond continued, completely disregarding his sister's actions, "all I ask is for thirty minutes of your time."

Kayla looked around, now finally aware that all eyes were on them like a reality show. She knew that they were waiting on her to react like a typical woman and attack Raymond. After deciding she was not going to give the people a show, she happened to turn her head and saw Bryan who for some odd reason was staring at her intensely. She had a sudden urge to run up to Bryan and kiss him right on the lips. It would have been the sweetest revenge for Raymond and his dumbass sister. She then put her focus back on Raymond who attempted to grab her hand. She decided to do something that would have everyone in the room guessing. She grabbed Raymond gently by the back of his neck, pressed her cheek against his cheek, and discreetly whispered in his ear, "I'm dead to you," as she pulled away and made her exit.

Kayla continued to replay the events in her mind as she walked back to the car. She started to think about what she should have said and how she really wanted to slap Erica. Mixed emotions began to fester as she tried to unravel why Raymond would hurt her and what she would do about it.

As she got in the car, she could not stop the tears from rolling down her cheeks.

The drive home was even worse. It was an emotional roller coaster for Kayla. She was still in shock because there was no sign that indicated that Raymond was ready to move on from the relationship. Sure, they had small arguments, but he was with her and Nicholas the majority of the time, told her he loved her constantly, and treated them like they were his small family. How could Raymond be so bold to a point where he felt comfortable bringing another woman to a gathering, knowing there was a possibility that Kayla could show up. If anything, he could have called and played it off by saying something important came up. Then, there was the fact Nicholas had gotten use to having Raymond being around.

After sitting in her driveway for over thirty minutes, she thought more about it and the more she thought about it, the faster the anger built. *Why should he be allowed to ride off in the sunset after being deceitful* she thought? "I can't believe I let that jackass off like that!" She screamed to herself, "That was so fucking weak of me." At that point, Kayla decided that she had definitely let Raymond off too easily. She put her car in reverse, backed out of her driveway, and headed back towards Raymond's home. As Kayla pulled up to the driveway, she noticed that all the guests had already left. She didn't even consider the fact that his family could have been still over, but since they were not, it made things a lot easier. She walked up to the door and politely rang the doorbell. Much to her surprise, Raymond answered the door.

"Kayla, I don't think this is a good time for you to be here right now," he said. His calm yet suspicious reaction made her even more eager to enter the home.

"Whatever," Kayla said pushing her way into the foyer.

"Kayla, I'm serious," he implemented in a sterner tone as he firmly grabbed her arm. She jerked away from his grasp only to hear yelling coming from the living room.

"Who the hell is that at my damn door!" yelled Mr. Jenson. At that point Kayla literally froze. She knew something was wrong because she had never heard or even heard of Mr. Jensen cursing.

"I told you to leave," Raymond said as he tried to push her back towards the front door, but it was too late.

"Oh, Katy, you're just in time dear," Mr. Jenson said as he rounded the corner. Mr. Jenson now smelled as if he had swam in whiskey and the fact that he couldn't remember her name screamed run. His eyes were fire red and his demeanor was frightening.

"Come on in, Kay," he forcefully insisted as he firmly grabbed Kayla by the arm.

"Dad, I think this is a family matter and-"

"Shut the hell up boy," he responded, totally disregarding his son's comment. Kayla looked back at Raymond who had a hopeless expression on his face.

"Sit down, Kathy, I want you to have a front seat of what a whore looks like," Mr. Jenson drunkenly stated as he practically placed Kayla on the zebra printed divan.

Kayla looked across the room at the horrifying sight of Mrs. Jenson balled up the corner of the living room with her face covered by her hands, crying uncontrollably.

"Dad, it's bad enough that you have to go about this in this manner, but company shouldn't be hearing our problems," Raymond reasoned.

Mr. Jenson let out a boisterous laugh saying, "Poor boy doesn't want people to find out his mom's a whore."

"Maybe it is a good idea that I leave," Kayla stammered, slowly attempting to get up.

"Sit your ass down, Kathy, you'll leave when I tell you to leave," he threatened, pointing to her.

"Dad, you need to chill out," Raymond said, walking towards his dad.

"Oh, oh, so your mom goes and fuck someone your age and disgraces herself as a wife…a mom…or any type of woman with professional decencies and a wife and here you are, a boy, trying to justify her!" he drunkenly screamed.

"No dad, I just feel that there's a better way to handle this without involving outsiders. Why don't we all sit down and discuss a way to work this out," Raymond reasoned.

Mr. Jenson paused, looked at his son, and then looked around the room. He then focused on Mrs. Jenson who was still in the corner sobbing.

"You know what, son, you're right. I'll show you exactly how I'm going to handle this." He staggered over and stood over Mrs. Jenson as if he was about to help her up.

He unexpectedly grabbed her by the hair and attempted to drag her from the corner. She started yelling in agony while Raymond ran across the room to his mom's aid and attempted to pull his dad from the tight hold.

"I'm going show this little cunt and that little cunt what happens when you sleep around," Mr. Jenson bellowed in drunken rage as he forcefully pushed Raymond to the floor with one arm. With the attention momentarily off her, Kayla made a quick dash towards the door and did not attempt to look back. She ran to her car and quickly locked the door. She fumbled with the keys as she put them into the ignition. Mr. Jenson was on a mission to hurt someone and it damn sure was not going to be her. She hurriedly accelerated out of the driveway towards her home. This was more than she had bargained for.

The drive home seemed like it took hours. Kayla quickly got out of the car, opened the front door, and promptly locked it. She did not know what was about to transpire from the events that took place that night. She knew no matter what the outcome was that night, someone at some point was going to get hurt. Luckily, her mom had Nicholas for the entire weekend. She could not help but to wish she had never went back to the house.

About 30 minutes later, after, undressing and still consumed by her thoughts, Kayla was startled at the sound of her cell phone ringing. She picked up the phone and noticed it was a call from Raymond. As much as Kayla wanted to know what happened, she dared not to pick up the phone.

She did not want to be a part of anything that could have possibly taken place. After a short pause, Raymond called back repeatedly, but Kayla refused to answer.

Finally settled into bed a few hours later with no further calls from Raymond, Kayla lied there sleeplessly, still paranoid about what went down in the Jenson's home. The whole situation put her in a weird position with Raymond, because she could not elaborate on the betrayal as she intended to. How could she talk about her relationship with him when his mom not only did the same thing to his dad, but with someone the same age as Raymond? Kayla had always joked with Raymond about how trendy Mrs. Jenson dressed in addition to her looking a decade younger than her real age. She wondered how and when did Mr. Jenson find out. Mr. Jenson did not seem like an abuser, but you never know what goes on behind closed doors. In theory, there had to be a reason why Mrs. Jenson stepped out on her husband. Kayla assumed that Mr. Jenson was boring and predictable opposed to the high energy and spontaneous young men that were probably hounding Mrs. Jenson. Kayla snickered at the thought of stiff Mr. Jenson trying to put a grove on his wife. Kayla's lewd thought was abruptly interrupted by the sound of repetitious thumps. She eased from her bed and walked slowly towards the noise. It was the front door. Someone was beating on her front door. The loud thuds from her heart made it seem as if it was about to drop out of her chest. She was so afraid that she could already feel the tears well up in her eyes. Without turning on the light, she peeked carefully out the window for a vehicle, but she did not see one.

The knocks grew louder and louder, but she dared not to open the door.

"Kayla, I know your in there, it's me, Raymond," he said in a shrill tone.

"Uh, it's kind of late Raymond," Kayla responded still talking to the door.

"Kayla, please…I'm begging you to let me in," he pleaded.

It sounded to Kayla like he was crying. She was almost tempted to tell him to go and find his side chick, but she decided to sympathize. She slowly unlocked the door leaving the chain on so she could peek out at Raymond. With tears rolling down his swollen eyes, he gripped his hand around the edge of the door. Kayla was petrified from the blood smudge left by his handprint.

Chapter 3

Kayla wasn't sure about what she should do next. There were a million questions swarming through her head and one always ensued because of the other. She wondered, *did Raymond's hand have his blood on it or his father's blood, or maybe even his mother's.* She left the scuffle hours ago, so why was there fresh blood on his hands? She knew that no matter what Raymond was about to tell her, someone got hurt and the situation was not over. She refused to let Raymond get her involved in a circumstance that did not have anything to do with her, especially since she caught him with another woman less than six hours ago. Although Kayla had a stern backbone and refused to be a pushover, she stood there terrified. The fact of the matter was that she was alone with a man who could not only over power her, but someone who had just went through a violent ordeal and could be full of rage as well as have an intent to harm. She had to figure out how to get them both away from her home and into a public setting.

She decided she would have to do something quick so he wouldn't have time to object to what she was saying or doing.

"Wait right here," she hurriedly said as she swiftly pushed his hand back while closing and locking the door.

"Kayla!" he yelled.

"Wait a minute, Raymond, I have to go and put on some clothes," she yelled back through the door. Surprisingly, he did not say anything as she eased back from the door. Her first thought was to go to her bedroom and locked the door, but Raymond could easily break through the window and do something dire before the police could make it there. She was trembling all over as she put on her jeans, a short navy blue jacket, and grabbed her keys. She had to straighten up and not let Raymond sense that she was afraid, if she didn't, she knew that he would try to control the situation.

She decided she would not even mention the blood on his hands or his parents. She was going to distract him with relationship things so she could control the situation. After getting dressed and grabbing her keys, she quickly opened the front door and shut it. Raymond was still standing on the porch looking disturbed.

"What are you doing?" he asked.

"We're going to get something to eat and you're going to tell me why you cheated," she demanded and walked towards her car.

"Follow me to Waffle House," she added. Raymond stood there unmoved by her attempt.

Kayla wasn't sure what Raymond would do next.

She was happy that she, at least, made it to the car where she felt safer than being in the house.

The driveway was slightly on the left side of the house, so she watched for the next few minutes through the passenger window where Raymond still stood unmoved and dazed. She wasn't sure what to do either, but she knew getting back out of the car wasn't an option. She cracked the window about a fourth of the way down and tried to get his attention.

"Well? Are you following me or not?"

"For what?" he yelled, "I'm not about to go with you to no damn restaurant," he replied angrily.

"And you're the one to be making all decisions now, right? She replied sarcastically.

"I'm not going to a fucking restaurant," he yelled.

"You need to keep your voice down before these nosy ass neighbors come outside."

"I don't have to do shit. Fuck you and your neighbors!"

"Well why in the hell…are you at my house? You can go and be with your little whore, I'm pretty sure she's open."

He briefly looked away and stood still for a minute while rubbing both hands over his face. Suddenly, he charged towards the car and violently kicked the passenger side door. Kayla was frighten to death as she started the car and began to hurriedly back out of the driveway. She stopped in the middle of the street and watched Raymond run from the driveway into the middle of the street like a mad man. He stood still and breathed heavily like a scene from a horror film. The yelling and hard thuds from Raymond kicking the side door must have wakened the next-door neighbors.

Once the neighbors turned on the porch light, Raymond instantly ran to his car, turned on the ignition, and sped off with squalling tires. Feeling like a bulldozer had been lifted from her shoulders, Kayla headed back in the house, slammed the front door, and made her way to the bedroom as she felled helplessly across the bed. She could not remember the last time she had dealt with so much drama in one night.

Kayla woke up late the next afternoon and prepared herself to go and get Nicholas. She made a conscious decision that Raymond would no longer be in her life and she would focus on her son and bettering her career. She knew that eventually, Nicholas would question Raymond's abstinence, so she tried to think of a mature answer that a child his age would understand. She gathered her thoughts as she walked out the door, suddenly, remembering the night before, she could feel her blood vessels bulging underneath her skin as she noticed three foot-sized dents on the passenger side of her car door. Her eyes begin to water and her fingers trembled as she dialed Raymond's number.

"What?" he answered almost yelling.

"Look, Raymond, I just stepped outside and noticed that you put three dents in my passenger door."

"Girl, I didn't do anything to your little car," he argued.

"Raymond!" she yelled, "you were kicking my car like a mad man last night, what do you mean it wasn't you?" she screamed.

"So what?"

"So, I'm going to need you to get your ass over here and pay for this damage or else I'll file a police report and get a statement from my neighbor who saw you," she argued, embellishing the truth.

"Look, my dad is in the hospital, so I really don't have time for this." He hung up. Kayla could care less if his dad was in a coma; she at least wanted Raymond to own up to what he had done and get it paid for. She attempted to call back several times, but he would not answer. She did not want to drive by his mom's house because she wasn't sure if he was there or what Mrs. Jenson condition was since he claimed his dad was in the hospital. For all she knew, Raymond could have been with the girl from the party and used his dad being in the hospital as an excuse to hurry and get off the phone. She decided to let things cool down a bit as well as calm herself down because she could not let her mother nor Nicholas see her upset. On the way over to her mom's house, all she could do was think about what she would do if Raymond would not fix her car.

She decided that if he did not pay for her car, he would pay for something else in return. Once Kayla pulled in front of her mother's driveway, she decided to back her car in so the passenger side would not face the house. As soon as she opened the door, she saw Nicholas playing on the floor and her mom was watching an old rerun of the Cosby Show. As always, Nicholas ran up to her with a big smile.

"Mommy!" he sung, "Look what I got," he said as he held up a red toy motorcycle.

"That's awesome baby, who bought it for you?" she asked, thinking she already knew the answer.

"My daddy," he grinned.

Kayla could feel her heart drop and skip a few beats all at once. She instantly looked at her mother, waiting for an explanation.

When the explanation was not instantly provided, she asked.

"What does he mean his daddy?"

"Yesterday afternoon someone knocked on the door, I opened it, and there Michael stood with a toy motorcycle in his hand."

"Where was Nicholas?"

"Here."

"Ma, I know that, did Nicholas see him?"

"Of course he did, you know this child will run to the door with you if he hears someone knocking."

"Well…what did he say?" Kayla continued to anxiously question. Kayla's mom took a deep breath as she grabbed the remote and changed the channel as if the conversation was frivolous.

"Mom?"

"Look," she interrupted before Kayla could continue, "he came over, said hello to Nicholas, I'm your daddy, and left a number for you to call him." Kayla's mother said as she pointed to the kitchen table. "I'm not interesting in discussing a man who doesn't take care of his child. Enough with the interrogation please."

It was too much information at once and Kayla was getting frustrated with her mother's short answers and nonchalant attitude. Nicholas had not seen his father since he was an infant, so this was a big deal to her since; technically, Nicholas just met his father for the first time.

She knew that her mom detested Michael, but regardless of their feelings, he was his dad. She went into the kitchen, grabbed the number, and then said her thanks and good-byes to her mother.

Kayla was festered with different emotions the entire ride home. She wondered what made Michael reach out after all this time and what she would say when they finally spoke? She also could not determine how she felt about him emotionally since this wasn't only the father of her child, but also a man she once truly loved. How long was he going to stick around this time, but even more importantly, what was Nicholas thinking? She did not want to bombard Nicholas with a hundred questions at once. She decided that the best time to talk to Nicholas would be that night before bed. She took a quick glance threw the rear view mirror at Nicholas who had dozed off with his motorcycle clutched tightly in his hand.

After making it home Kayla straighten the house and prepared dinner while Nicholas watched cartoons. She wasn't sure if she would contact Michael that night or wait a few days, but she knew she had to for the sake of her son. She assumed that Nicholas would run in the kitchen and bombard her with a million questions about his dad, but he didn't. Even though he acted like he hadn't seen Michael earlier, he held on to that motorcycle as if it was glued to his hand. As she sat at the dinner table with Nicholas, a thousand different scenarios ran through her mind about how the conversation would go between her and Michael. She was not sure if she should talk to him over the phone or have the talk face to face.

She thought about waiting until Nicholas was at daycare or with his grandmother just in case she couldn't control her emotions or things got out of hand. After washing up and getting Nicholas into his bed, she decided to go ahead and have the talk with him.

"Did my little man have fun with Grandma this weekend?" she asked.

"Yes, mommy. Grandma took me to the park to feed the ducks."

"Wow! I bet that was fun."

"Yes, and I watched the girl fall down on her butt at the slide," he giggled.

"Oh, okay, so did you talk to your daddy yesterday."

"Yes, mommy, he bought me this motorcycle and said he loved me and was coming to see me."

"Oh…okay baby, well, goodnight and I'll see you in the morning."

"Okay, mommy, goodnight, I love you."

Kayla didn't know what to think. She knew she was not a child psychologist, but she felt that Nicholas was associating his daddy's love with that motorcycle. She knew that Nicholas was too young to comprehend that his daddy was suppose to be around frequently, but she wondered, *by Nicholas seeing his dad did he realize his abstinence or did he even care?* Perhaps he was just content with the fact that the man, who said that he was his daddy, bought him a new motorcycle. Kayla hadn't talked about Michael much, because she wanted Nicholas to be older so he could understand better.

Kayla sat down for a few more minutes and finally decided to call Michael, but a call came through to her instead.

"Hello…Kayla?" said the female voice.

"Mrs. Jenson?" she questioned recognizing the voice.

"Hi, Kayla, can we talk a minute?" Ms. Jenson asked sounding distraught.

"Uh…yeah, sure Ms. Jenson," she hesitantly responded.

"I wanted to apologize about what happened the other night. I know things sort of got out of hand. It was the last thing I expected from Jimmy."

What did she mean 'got out of hand,' Kayla sarcastically thought, *Mr. Jenson had you balled-up screaming in a corner.*

"Oh…it's fine," Kayla finally responded as she brushed off her thought.

"So…how is Nicholas?"

"He's fine," Kayla suspiciously answered. *Who switches gears that fast and what in the hell was Ms. Jenson's motive* she wondered?

"Uh… look, Ms. Jenson, I'm not trying to be rude and I appreciate the call, but was there something in particular that you wanted to discuss?"

"No…no," she stammered, "Well, actually, I kind of do have something to discuss. You see, Raymond was out of control after you left…uh…I was wondering, well, did he come see you or talk to you that night?"

Kayla didn't know what Ms. Jenson was fishing for, but something just was not right.

"He called a few times, but I was extremely upset, of course, I would be, considering, he had another woman over. Just out of curiosity, did you know about the other woman, Ms. Jenson?"

"Of course not honey, you know I wouldn't get into you kids' business. That was the last thing I expected from Raymond."

Did she just contradict her answer? Kayla thought.

"Well, it was nice speaking with you Ms. Jenson, but I'm getting ready for bed."

"Oh…that's fine, I'm sorry to keep you up. Oh, one last thing please, Kayla, if Raymond contacts you, let him know that we love him and we're still here for him."

That last statement dumbfounded Kayla. What did she mean let Raymond know we love him and who was the "we" she was referring to? Had she and Mr. Jenson reconciled already? Kayla decided it was time for her to fish for some answers. Besides, Raymond mentioned Mr. Jenson being in the hospital, so Kayla wanted to find out if this was true.

"Should I call you or Mr. Jenson?" Kayla finally questioned. The short awkward silence seemed as if it lasted for five minutes.

"Uh…well, Mr. Jenson…" without finishing her statement, the phone hung up.

Chapter 4

The next morning Kayla was getting ready to take Nicholas to the daycare and then head off to work, but she couldn't help but think about the weird call from Mrs. Jenson. After speaking with her, she didn't even feel like having the conversation with Michael; she was just too concerned with what was going on with Raymond. Something happened the other night after the party and, in some way or the other, Mrs. Jenson assumed Kayla knew something. Furthermore, why did Mrs. Jenson hang up at the mention of Mr. Jenson, or Jimmy as she called him? Mrs. Jenson could have just brushed off the question with a simple response, but Kayla had a feeling that Mrs. Jenson wanted to know if Raymond had told her anything about that night. Bothered by the entire situation, Kayla could not resist the temptation that dwelled within. She decided that as soon as she dropped Nicholas off at daycare, she would attempt to give Raymond another call.

After waving her goodbyes to her son, Kayla quickly got back in the car and dialed Raymond before leaving the parking lot. She decided that she would not tell Raymond about the call from his mother. She allowed the phone to ring five times, but still no answer. Just as she was about to hang up, Raymond answered.

"Why are you calling me?" he asked in an aggravated tone.

"What?" Kayla questioned confusingly. *Is this jackass serious* she thought? It literally threw her off her entire approach.

"I thought I told you I didn't want to see your number across my phone ever again!" he raged.

"Look, Jackass! You owe me for these dents in my car and until you pay, you will hear from me every got damn day!" Kayla screamed.

"You would do anything to try and turn me into your baby daddy. I don't want you or Nicholas, Kayla. Did you see that woman who I was with the other night? That's were my heart is, with a child free woman."

"I hate you and I hope you burn in hell, Raymond." Kayla retaliated as she quickly hung up the phone swerving back into her lane. She couldn't remember the last time she was so infuriated. She burst into tears as she hit her stirring wheel several times.

"That arrogant bastard!" she yelled. She pulled up into the employee parking area of the hospital. As she wiped her face and put eye drops in her eyes to cover the redness, she repeated what Raymond had said in her mind. *How could he be so heartless?* She thought.

She knew Raymond was capable of many things, but that was the last thing she had expected him to say. She put her face in her hands and started crying all over again.

Kayla finally pulled herself together and headed into the hospital. She clocked in and checked her schedule for her daily rounds. After grabbing her assigned charts, she headed down to the meeting hall where all nurses in her assigned group met at the beginning of the shift. Trying to remain as unnoticeable as possible, she sat in the back hoping the usual busy bodies and talkers would go to their normal seats. Sure enough, Destiny, another practical nurse in her group flopped down beside her and began talking instantly.

"So, you know that married guy I was talking to, right? He had the nerve to get mad at me, because I brought up my other guy friend's name. Unbelievable, right?" she questioned, waiting for Kayla's response.

"Look, Destiny, I had a long weekend and I need a minute to collect my thoughts, okay?"

"Well, excuse me, I didn't know this was Ms. Kayla's world," she sarcastically responded as she got up and walked off.

Kayla did not feel like the drama today. Besides, Destiny was not a close friend or anything. She was just someone who liked to tell all of her personal business to make herself seem popular or important. Normally, Kayla would shoot the breeze and try to give her advice and helpful comments to aid in the particular drama at hand, but Destiny never really applied the advice, so Kayla definitely refused to waste her breath today.

As the head nurse went over patient information, room orders, and prescriptions, Kayla sat there thinking about all the times that Raymond had told her she was his everything and how his world would not turn without her in it.

Work was long and drawn out. Kayla could not focus on her assignments, so she ended up going to the wrong rooms and checking on the wrong patients. Kayla's supervisor knew that this was highly unlike Kayla, so she knew something was bothering her. On Kayla's lunch break, the supervisor came over to Kayla's lunch table to let her know she wouldn't have to work back shift. Back shift meant they would have to stay three extra hours to help with the late night emergency room staff. Kayla was relieved and thanked her. The rest of her night went better as she decided how she was going to counteract Raymond's insults.

It was now midnight as Kayla walked toward the car garage after clocking off her shift. She decided to go home and rest then, perhaps, speak to Raymond's mom to see if she could talk some sense into him before she got the police involved about her damaged door. Just as she was about to get in the car, she was startled by Destiny's hand shutting her door.

"Bitch, what is wrong with you?" Kayla protested after spinning around looking into Destiny's face.

"I don't appreciate you acting brand new today like you better than somebody." Destiny protested.

"Destiny, I got a lot of shit going on right now and I don't need to be involved with extra drama," Kayla kindly, but firmly, explained.

"What do you mean drama? Your son is a bastard child and you have the nerve to say I'm drama?" Destiny exclaimed, raising her voice and stepping closer to Kayla.

Kayla went from being aggravated to pissed. Her nostrils flared as she stepped closer now chest to chest with Destiny.

"If you ever, in your life, step in my face about anything, I don't give a damn what it is, I put it on my life you'll regret it."

"Is that a threat?" she carefully challenged back.

"No, bitch, this is a promise and a pleasure."

Kayla could see fear in Destiny's face as she walked off and said whatever. For some reason, Kayla didn't feel justified. This tramp was sleeping with a married man and she had the audacity to call her son a bastard! Kayla was furious. She knew what she would do to get back at Destiny, but her rage didn't stop there. She wanted to release some anger. This was the second time someone had offended her in regards to her innocent child and that incident was the straw that broke the camel's back. Thinking back to earlier, she decided to pay Raymond a visit.

After stopping by the store to pick up a few supplies, Kayla headed to Raymond's home. As late as it was, she figured everyone would probably be settled inside. She parked on the street over just as she did for the party. She grabbed the supplies from her bag, put on the gloves, and crept into view of the driveway. As she slowly walked towards Raymond's car parked in the front lawn, she could feel the perspiration on her forehead as she kneeled low beside the tire and pulled out a few nails.

She anxiously looked around for a minute as she considered aborting her mission. She decided she would not turn back now. Raymond needed a taste of his own medicine.

Kayla took two nails and placed them directly underneath the front and back tires. That way, once Raymond backed out the driveway, the nails would pierce into the tires. She wanted to do all four, but she figured that would look too suspicious. Just as the satisfaction of victory had overcome her face, Kayla suddenly saw the porch light come on.

She ducked beside Raymond's car as she peeked to see who came outside. Her heart was heavily pounding as she saw Raymond and his mother step out onto the front patio. She heard Raymond tell his mother that she shouldn't drive in her condition. Mrs. Jenson insisted that she was okay and not to worry. Kayla felt her stomach turn. She knew she was caught red handed. She had nowhere to hide, so all she could do was run as fast as she could. After a few more minutes of verbal volleyball, Raymond finally said he was going back in the house to get his keys. After she saw Mrs. Jenson follow him, Kayla quickly grabbed her bag and ran as fast as she could. She prayed that they hadn't came back out of the house and seen her running away. Once Kayla got in her car, she fumbled with the keys and pulled off as fast as she could.

During the drive home, Kayla could still feel her body shaking from her scheme. She felt nervous, excited, and justified all at the same time. As late as it was, she was hoping that no one in Raymond's neighborhood saw her car. She tried to figure out where Mrs. Jenson intended on going so late.

Wherever it was, she definitely didn't want Raymond to know and Raymond was doing everything he could to stop her.

Once she got home, she settled in so she could get up early to pick Nicholas up from her mom's house and take him to school. As soon as she got in bed and turned off the light, her cell phone rang. Her heart started rapidly beating because she knew it was Raymond calling to tell her that someone had seen her. Kayla looked down at her phone at the unknown number on her screen. It was a local area code, so she figured it was someone she knew calling from someone else's phone.

"Hello," she answered.

"What are you doing?" The voice responded. Kayla didn't recognize the person calling her that late at night.

"Who is this?" Kayla anxiously asked.

"This is Bryan, from the party."

"Bryan?" She asked. "Why are you calling me this late and how did you get my number."

"I took it out of Raymond's phone when I asked to use it the other day," he promptly responded.

"Why would you do that and again, why are you calling me this late?"

"Look, Kayla, I know you don't know me and I apologize for calling you this late. The only reason why I called this late is because Erica told me you worked as a nurse, so I figured you'd be up in the wee hours."

"Why would she tell you that," Kayla suspiciously asked.

"Well, that night after the party she couldn't stop talking about you."

"Right, I'm sure it was all wonderful things," she replied with sarcasm.

"Yeah, well, I knew she was upset and probably jealous that you're doing something with your life or maybe she didn't like the fact you were stealing her brother away from her."

"Well, apparently, I'm not the one she should be worried about."

"So, are you and Raymond officially broken up?"

"Bryan, I am a little more interested in knowing why my ex-boyfriend sister's boyfriend is asking me these question."

"Erica isn't my girlfriend and to be totally honest with you, I think she may be bi-sexual."

"Why would you say that, she must have turned you down?"

"Of course not," he answered, sounding offended, "we have never even taken it there. Were just good friends."

"That's nice, so did you call to tell me that Erica was talking bad about me or to ask about Raymond and me?"

"Neither, actually. I wanted to see if you were okay and maybe I could take you to lunch sometime."

"That's very sweet of you, Bryan, but I'm not interested in getting involved with anyone, especially not someone close to Erica, no offense."

"Well, if you ever decided you want to have lunch, strictly as friends, my door is open."

"Thank you and thanks for calling."

"No problem, hope to hear from you soon, Kayla."

After she hung up, she wondered why Bryan was desperate enough to steal her number out of Raymond's phone. Had Erica said something to him about her that actually turned him on? Furthermore, why would Bryan say she was bi-sexual? There had to have been some incident or a particular reason why he would make that accusation. Bryan was charming and gorgeous, so why would she reject him or why would he have to lie? She wanted to know more dirt on Erica just in case she had another run in with her. She started to think twice about taking Bryan up on his lunch invitation.

After taking Nicholas to school the next day, Kayla headed to work in a good mood. She started to feel flattered that Bryan went out of his way to get her number. She pulled into the parking lot and decided to save the number that he had called her from last night. Once she signed into the meeting room, her supervisor told them that the morning meeting was cancelled and she was only giving out the daily routes. Kayla knew that something was wrong, because she noticed some of her co-workers glancing at her from time to time. After the last route was given, Kayla was empty-handed. Everyone left the room as Kayla sat there.

While leaving, a few of the other female nurses, including Destiny, looked back at Kayla and shook their heads. The supervisor closed the door and sat down in front of her.

"Kayla, I respect your work, you always do a good job on your shift, and you do not have any attendance issues. As hard as it is for me to say this, you will have to be reassigned."

"What? Why?"

"A co-worker came to me in confidentiality and told me you threaten her. You know that is not tolerated and is grounds for dismissal."

"Someone is trying to get me fired, Ms. Hawkins, because the last thing I would do is threaten someone. I have a child at home to take care of."

"Kayla, I believe you and that's why you're not fired, but I have to reassign you to another department until the investigation is complete."

The supervisor gave Kayla her new floor assignment along with the paperwork and told her to report to the area immediately. Once she walked down the hall, she saw Destiny who was staring her eye to eye with a smirk on her face. Kayla felt the anger build in her body as she thought about grabbing her and choking her to death as she passed her. She could not believe that Destiny would set her up and try to get her fired. Kayla couldn't believe that after all the advice she gave to Destiny that she would stoop to this level. She even consoled her when Destiny cried over the married man she was screwing. The more Kayla thought about it, she remembered Destiny telling her the married man's wife name and the restaurant where the wife worked. She even told Kayla when and where she would meet the husband to mess around. Kayla then paused, looked back at Destiny who happened to be still looking at her, and gave her a mischievous smirk. Revenge would never taste so sweet.

Chapter 5

Assigned to the women's surgery unit as an assistant, Kayla spent the majority of her night getting to know her new supervisor, Gabby, and new team members. To her surprise, she liked the new area because the time went by quickly since there was always something going on. The atmosphere wasn't uptight or too demanding like her previous floor. The nurses seemed more down to earth and relaxed. Most of the nurses were about five to seven years her senior, so that was probably what made the difference. The only thing that she didn't like about her new area is that sometimes she would get sent down to the trauma unit to help distribute meds for patients as well as change their urinary or IV bags. Down in the trauma area patients go from being stable to unstable at the drop of a dime, so no one knew what to expect.

Just as Kayla was ending her shift, a tenured nurse asked if she could deliver one more dose of meds to a patient in trauma. Kayla knew that it wasn't her responsibility to do it, so she asked whom did the chart belong to originally. The nurse told her an excuse about someone getting sick, but Kayla figured that a few of the older nurses would try to coerce her into extra work. As tired as Kayla was, she didn't feel like having an altercation on her first day on the new assignment. She had just been transferred, so she didn't want her new team thinking she was the troublemaker. She reluctantly agreed and took the chart from the nurse's hand. She went back to her follow-up chart and noted in detail what the nurse had asked of her so Gabby could sign off on it. It wasn't that Kayla was trying to be a snitch; she wanted to make sure that no one else was trying to set her up.

When she took the chart to Gabby, she awkwardly looked at Kayla and told her not to make it a habit because the tenured nurses may try to pull that often. Kayla felt a great deal of relief that someone, at least, acted as if she cared about fairness. Kayla took the slip from the chart and went to get the required medication. After reading over the instructions, she matched the chart with the room and pulled the file that was on the wall beside the door. Once she opened the file, she rumbled through the pages to make sure the medicine, room, and patient matched. Kayla almost dropped the chart as she gasped when she noticed Jimmy Jenson as the patient on the inside cover. Kayla was extremely nervous and she didn't know what to do.

She thought that it truly was a setup, but no one at that hospital could have known the association between her and Mr. Jenson. Out of all rooms and stations in the hospital that Kayla could have been assigned to, she somehow had gotten Mr. Jenson who wasn't even on her charts. It was just a twist of irony that Kayla was faced to deal with at the time.

She looked around as she slowly opened the door and peeked in at Mr. Jenson. He was laying there on the bed with his head wrapped in a thick cloth. She quietly stepped in and lightly closed the door. As she tiptoed toward the edge of his bed, she noticed that Mr. Jenson was sound asleep with an oxygen mask and several other tubes extending from his body. She placed the meds on the table and reopened the file to see if she could find any information on his injuries. The back worksheet had an illustration of a severe wound to the cranium, but labeled him in a temporary stable condition.

After looking at Mr. Jenson's condition, Kayla felt horrible about what she had done to Raymond's tires. She felt more horrible about when she called Raymond regarding the dents in her door and said to herself that she didn't care if Mr. Jenson was in a coma. She had no idea that Raymond was dealing with that type of burden. She tried her best not to sob. As she added the medication to Mr. Jenson's IV, she wondered how he sustained the injury. The last thing she remembered was Raymond attempting to pull his dad off his mom and how he showed up at her house with blood on his hands. She checked all of the monitors and made sure his breathing was regular before exiting the room.

Finally done with her shift, Kayla went down to the locker area to grab her things. Although the floor change was unexpected, she liked the change and the fact that she could occasionally check on Mr. Jenson. She wasn't sure if she was going to let Raymond know that she could keep him current on his dad's condition. She felt uneasy about the entire situation now that she knew that Raymond wasn't lying about his dad. Not wanting to be bombarded with questions from nurses on her old team, Kayla decided to walk through the main lobby instead of the side exit. Just as she was walking out, Raymond was walking in the lobby.

Kayla felt even more awkward once they finally made eye contact. She froze in place as Raymond slowly walked towards her with his hands in his pockets.

"Hey," he nervously said.

"Hello, Raymond," she awkwardly responded, recalling their last heated conversation.

"For the record, I want to apologize. I didn't mean what I said. I'm just stressed and worried, so I came up here to see pops."

"Oh, of course, apology accepted and I apologize as well for yelling at you about the dents…He's doing fine," she quickly added, while fidgeting with her fingers.

"You've seen him today?" he asked.

"Well, he was my last round. I didn't even know it was your dad until I picked up the charts. Is this your first time visiting him?"

"Yeah, I had to force myself to come because I didn't want to see him lying in a hospital bed."

"Yeah, I guess this entire ordeal must be pretty hard on your family."

"Life has a funny way of throwing curve balls. I would have never expected my mom having an affair and now this."

Kayla couldn't believe that Raymond was that naïve. Mr. and Mrs. Jenson acted as if they were father and daughter oppose to wife and husband.

"What did they say?" he asked, breaking into her thoughts.

"Who?"

"The charts, what did the charts say?" he anxiously questioned.

"Nothing terrible, they said it was a concussion, but he is in stable condition."

With a sigh of relief, Raymond rolled back his eyes and gently put his arms around her. He held her as if she had told him she saved his dad's life.

"Thank you, for being there, Kayla. I know now he will be in good hands."

"You don't have to thank me," she weakly smiled not knowing what else to say.

"Of course, I do. I know this isn't the time to talk about this, but I know I did you wrong and I've been acting like an ass lately."

"People make mistakes, Raymond, its okay."

"No, Kayla, you were good to me, you never did me wrong, and now I'm dealing with a woman who lies and flatten my tires for no reason, well, I did lie, but still this girl is crazy."

After realizing he was still with the other woman, Kayla's remorse slowly progressed to resentment. She didn't mind that he blamed the other girl for flattening his tires. To her, it served him right for cheating on her in the first place.

"Well, I'm working close to the trauma unit, so from time to time I can check on your dad and report his status."

"That would be amazing. Thank you so much, Kayla," he said as he gave her another hug. "And I'm sorry about the dents I put in your car door. I guess you really do reap what you sow."

"That's what they say." She softly added.

"My dad's brother fixes dents, I'm not sure if you met him before, but I can call him tomorrow and see when he can fix yours and I'll pay him." She agreed and then gave Raymond directions to his dad's room.

They parted ways as Raymond headed up the hall and Kayla out the door. She walked to the parking garage and got in the car thinking about what Raymond said about his new girlfriend. Even if Raymond did think the new girlfriend destroyed his tires, lied, or whatever, he still hadn't left the woman alone. She was still highly upset that he cheated in the first place. Perhaps the only reason why he was even being nice to her was that he knew she was someone he could trust to keep an eye on his dad.

Kayla woke up the next day feeling moody, still consumed with the previous day's events. She was happy that Raymond agreed to fix her car, but still bothered by the fact that he admitted to currently dating the woman that he cheated on her with.

If it wasn't for Destiny, she wouldn't be in that unit in the first place. Kayla was still upset with the fact that Destiny intended to get her fired. Her frustration was intense, so instead of letting the issue subside, she decided to go and pay Destiny's cheating boy toy's wife a visit.

The restaurant Destiny mentioned was downtown in an upscale area. As she pulled up in the parking lot, she wasn't sure how she would approach Tameka since women were so catty.

She had never seen her before, but she could identify her by the name tag and with a name like Tameka, she knew she had to have been a black woman. When she walked in, she asked the hostess if Tameka was working the bar area, hoping to get some type of information from the hostess. The hostess informed her that Tameka was working on the floor in the patio section. Kayla spotted a high top table in the bar area and decided to sit down. She took a small piece of paper and wrote:

Your Husband has a double life. If you want to catch him, He meets his mistress every other Thursday at the Hilton Inn on Walnut Street.

She folded the note and wrapped a two-dollar tip around it. She went around to the opposite side of the restaurant and stopped another waitress.

"Excuse me, ma'am, do you know Tameka?"

"Yes, she's out on the patio," she hurriedly responded.

"This is my first time eating here and I was wondering what the normal gratuity was?" Kayla asked, so the server wouldn't become suspicious.

"Oh, it's usually 10 to 20% of the bill."

"Oh, great, I'm not sure where I was sitting so could you give this to her, I'm in a big hurry."

"No problem," the waitress agreed as she walked off towards the patio.

Kayla quickly went outside and watched the waitress give the note to a short, thick light-skinned woman with long black hair pulled to the back. Tameka immediately stuck the tip in her pocket and continued with her guest.

Kayla pulled off the lot thinking about how Tameka would feel once she read the note. She knew Tameka would be asking the waitress what the person who gave her the note looked like. She began to feel guilty, because she knew it would be one of the worse days of Tameka's life. What if there were children involved in the midst of it all? Then again, Kayla began to justify her actions because it was wrong for Tameka's husband to be sleeping around with a slut anyway.

By the end of the week, Kayla was exhausted from pulling double shifts at the hospital. She hadn't seen Nicholas all week, nor had she heard of any developing stories on Destiny and the cheating husband. She thought maybe Tameka took the money and didn't pay attention to the note that was wrapped inside. As she was ending yet another overworked night at the hospital, she looked at her cell phone, noticing two missed calls from a number she didn't recognize. Her heart fluttered at the possibility of it being Tameka from the restaurant, but how would Tameka know it was her who left the note, and furthermore, how would she be able to get her number.

She assumed it couldn't be Tameka as she walked outside and called the number.

"Hello," the male voice answered.

"Yeah, someone called this number twice and I was trying to see who it was," she responded.

"Hey, Kayla, this is Michael."

"Michael? Wow! I haven't heard from you in a while. I didn't recognize your voice." Michael was the last person she had expected to be on the other end of her phone.

"What have you been up to?" He asked.

"Nothing much, just working and taking care of our son Nicholas," she chimed as she got in the car.

"Oh, I came by your mom's house the other day. Did she tell you?"

"Yeah, she told me."

"I left my number for you to call me, did she give it to you?"

"Yes...she did."

"Okay, am I missing something? Why didn't you call?"

"Michael, I have a lot going on. I hadn't spoken to you in at least two and a half years, so I honestly need some time to soak it all in."

"I guess I can't blame you for that. How has he been?"

"He's been good. He's healthy and he somehow has your silly personality."

"For real?" He laughed. "How do you figure that?"

"I just know. He likes to make people laugh by doing and saying silly things just like you."

"I can't wait to see him again," he said, still laughing.

Kayla paused, because she didn't know how to respond to his last comment about seeing Nicholas. The last thing she wanted was for Nicholas to have some father who would be in and out of his life.

"Why now?" Kayla finally asked.

He sighed. "Look, Kayla, I know I haven't been around and I have been a terrible dad basically since Nicholas was born. I decided to leave the streets alone; I have a real job, and want to be in my son's life."

"It took you two years to realize this?"

"I didn't call you to argue and for you to make me feel like I'm shit. I called you to build some type of open communication so I can see my son."

"Don't get mad at me for being cautious, okay. You are the one who left me high and dry to raise our son by myself," she argued as tears welled in her eyes.

"I'm sorry, Kayla, I truly am. As a man, I can admit to my mistakes. I'm sorry. But if you can't forgive me for my mistakes and accept the fact that I am here now trying to be in my son's life, then we're back where we started."

She took a deep breath as she let a tear roll down her cheek. She had been waiting on this conversation for a long time.

"I get a full day off this Saturday, so if you're not busy, maybe we can take Nicholas to Fun World or something."

"That sounds good. Give me a call once you two get ready, I'll get directions to your house and we can go from there."

After agreeing to the arrangement, Kayla hung up the phone and sighed, because a huge burden had been released from her shoulders. She was still cautious about Michael's true intentions, but she was thrilled that Nicholas would finally get to spend time his dad. Now, all she had to do is work on any personal feelings that may still be festering inside her regarding Michael.

Chapter 6

It was Saturday afternoon and the beautiful spring sky produced sunrays through the cirrostratus clouds that hovered above. Kayla and Nicholas were getting ready for their day with Michael for the first time ever. Michael agreed to come and pick them up, so they could grab some lunch and take Nicholas to the park. Although she wanted to make the day primarily about Nicholas spending time with his dad, she also made sure that she was on her "A" game as well. She decided to wear her blue jean skinny jeans and dark brown ankle boots that matched her brown off-the-shoulder top. She pulled her hair back in order to accentuate the effort she put into her flawless make-up and to show off the black-dotted feathered earrings she wore. After one last check of herself in the mirror, she went into Nicholas's room and made sure he was ready to go.

Arriving at the house thirty minutes later, Michael walked in wearing a polo shirt and jeans. He looked even more handsome now that he had gotten a low haircut. Since she last saw him, he gained a few pounds, which complimented his tall slender frame.

"Are you ready to hangout with your dad?" he asked Nicholas as he rubbed him on top of his head.

"Yes!" Nicholas excitedly responded.

"You look nice," Michael said now turning his attention to Kayla.

"Thanks, I know," she joked.

"I was thinking we should go eat first, because a brother hungry."

"Well, a sister and a kid hungry too so let's go," Kayla responded as they both laughed.

By the time they arrived at the restaurant and sat at the table, everything seemed normal. Michael was making conversation with Kayla and Nicholas as if he had been around them since Nicholas was born. Kayla didn't feel the awkward tension that she assumed she would have due to Michael not being around those few years. Although things were going well with Nicholas was around, she knew that there would be an adult conversation soon to come.

After lunch, they headed to the park as planned. Kayla took a seat on the park bench while Michael walked with Nicholas over to the huge outdoor jungle gym. She watched as Nicholas happily enjoyed the company of his father until Nicholas decided to blend in with other boys of his age. Michael slowly walked towards the bench were Kayla was sitting as he occasionally looked back making sure Nicholas was okay.

"He reminds me of me so much when I was a kid," Michael began.

"I know, right, you two look exactly alike on the old photos I saw over to your dad's home."

"Did my dad or mom try to contact you when I was away?"

"No, I figured since you didn't want anything to do with us that they felt the same way."

"No, Kayla, I don't feel that way. They used to ask me about Nicholas all the time and I would tell them that he was doing good because I know the type of woman you are."

"Look, you don't have to make it sound good, Michael, just say that you didn't want anything to do with us, because you already had another baby on the way."

Michael took a deep breath and sighed. "Yes, I do have a little girl around Nicholas's age, but no, we aren't a family. I was being young and stupid, so I slipped and had Mia."

Kayla wasn't sure how she felt at that moment. It was one thing assuming he had a child, but another thing when he actually admitted to it.

"I guess Mia is the child who had the opportunity to know her dad and her dad's family while my son got rejection," she angrily said as tears came to her eyes.

"Kayla, stop," he said as he grabbed her and put his arms around her. "I did some terrible things back in the day and I'm sorry. I treated you horribly and I could never make up for the valuable time I've lost with my son. Just please give me another chance to be here for you two."

"Michael, don't say you'll be here for me. Just say you'll be here for Nicholas and help out the best way you can."

"Okay, I can do that."

There was an awkward moment of silence between them as they watch Nicholas play with his new friends. Nicholas excitedly ran over to give his mom a hug.

"Mommy, I'm having fun with my new friends."

"That's great, baby, make sure you be careful, okay?"

"Okay, mommy, hey mommy, can Raymond come to the park next time with daddy?"

In shock, Kayla wasn't sure how to respond. "Well, Nicholas, let's just have fun for now and we'll talk about it later."

"Okay, Mommy," he agreed, hugging her again and ran off.

She couldn't make eye contact with Michael, because the moment was now even more awkward. It wasn't that she had to explain anything to him; it was just the fact that she was still embarrassed about the breakup with Raymond.

"Who is this Raymond guy?" Michael finally asked.

"He's my ex-boyfriend."

"He can't be too much of an ex if Nicholas still thinks he can see him."

"Who are you to question me about anything?"

"I'm his father."

"Since when, today?"

"Alright, Kayla, things are getting heated and I don't want to turn our first outing into a World War IV. I want you to know that I'm not playing father, I AM HIS FATHER."

"I'll try to work on changing my attitude for the sake of Nicholas because I don't want him to see us going at it every time we are together," she replied.

"That's a start. We will take it one day at a time and hopefully I can work my way into Nicholas's heart. The last thing I want is for him to depend on another man to be his dad."

"Truce?"

"Truce," he agreed as they shook on it.

When Michael arrived back at Kayla's home, Nicholas was in the backseat fast asleep. Michael picked him up and carried him in the house. He laid Nicholas on his bed and walked out of the bedroom gently closing the door behind him.

"I had a good time with you two," he said, sitting beside Kayla in the living room.

"Yeah, I think Nicholas had the most fun of all," she giggled.

"I know, right. He is so silly and smart."

"He gets his smarts from me, but he is silly like you." She teased.

"When do you think I could see you two again?"

"Well, my hours are crazy at the hospital, so I don't want to set up a specific time and I end up working."

"I'm off on weekends, so how about you let me know the next weekend you're off and we can plan something then. In the meantime, is it okay if I call to see how you two are doing?"

"You better," she laughed as she got up to walk him out the door.

He gave her that amazing smile that he gave when they first started dating and hugged her tightly before walking out the door. She closed the door feeling confused by the fact that she still had feelings for him. She sat on the couch still in disbelief about him having another child the same age as Nicholas. All those times he told her that he loved her and how she was the only one was a bold face lie.

If he lied and deceived her then, how would she know he wasn't doing the exact same thing now?

A few weeks had past and Michael had called almost every other day to check on Nicholas. He seemed genuine in his pursuit to stay a constant in Nicholas's life. Michael even took Nicholas over to his mother's house, so she and his family members could get to know him. He also asked Kayla out for dinner and a movie, so they could have fun for old time sake. Kayla had turned down his first few attempts, but after a while, Michael's persistence paid off. Kayla had the upcoming Friday off, so she had planned for Nicholas to stay with Michael's mother in order to give her mother a break.

It was Monday afternoon and Kayla had arrived to work feeling great. Her work team had taken a liking to her, so she wasn't having any more problems with them. She also had a constant set of patients that she dealt with, opposed to having different patients everyday as it was in her old department. At lunch, Kayla sat with her team discussing medical procedures when an old teammate from her other department came and said she wanted to talk to her in private.

"Kayla, you will never believe what happened," assistant nurse, Rebecca, said as Kayla followed her to a private area.

"Destiny is here in the hospital in critical condition."

"What!" Kayla gasped.

"Girl, yes! You know that everyone around here knew she was messing with a married man, so somehow, the wife found out, but that's not the sick part. Supposedly, the wife and the husband ended up tying her up, raping her, and then beating her."

"You're lying!" Kayla exclaimed.

"She is in section B1 of the intensive care unit. You can go see for yourself, and oh, don't tell anyone that I told you," Rebecca said, walking off.

Kayla didn't move. She was trying to process the information in her head. Rebecca had to have been exaggerating, she was known for doing that. Then again, maybe Rebecca was seeing how Kayla would react to the news knowing that Destiny was the one who had gotten her transferred. She wondered was Rebecca trying to see if Kayla was involved. However, Rebecca couldn't stand Destiny either, since Destiny had slept with her ex-boyfriend, so she knew Rebecca hadn't reformed. She decided to go down to the ICU and see for herself.

Kayla waited until midnight before going down to the ICU. She knew that there would be superior staff swarming everywhere had she went during her lunch. She held warm blankets in her hands, in case a staff member in the ICU asked if she was charted for the area. She looked around in the B1 section, but there was no sign of Destiny. With a small sigh of relief, she walked towards the D1 section where the ICU ended. Just as she was about to walk out of the double doors, the room on the right side of her had a partially cracked door where she could see a propped leg in a cast. It was Destiny. Destiny's leg was in a white cast along with her arm. One of her eyes was swollen and she had a white cloth bandaged wrapped around her head just as Mr. Jenson did.

As Kayla had gotten closer to the opened door, she noticed that Destiny's lip was swollen as well.

The rest of her body was wrapped in thick white covers. Kayla felt horrible as a tear rolled down her cheek. She quickly left the scene feeling distraught about what she had done. She couldn't believe that Destiny was dealing with people who were animals! Never in a million years did she expect that to have happen. She thought, *how did Rebecca know that they raped her, was that something Destiny told the nurses, or something that Rebecca fabricated.* Judging from appearance, Tameka didn't seem like the type of woman who rapes another woman. It was rare that she heard a black woman raping a white woman in their small town. Kayla assumed that the race card was being pulled somewhere in this tragedy. Kayla went to sit down in the break-room in order to get her thoughts together.

"You look sad," said one of the nurses as she walked in and saw Kayla's face.

"Yeah, it's a sad day," Kayla replied.

"Oh, so, I guess you heard too?"

"Yeah, I did, wait, how did you know, Destiny?"

"Destiny? Who is that?" asked the nurse.

"I thought that's who we were talking about."

"Oh, no, sweetheart. It's Mr. Jenson, the man I charted you on that night. He was pronounced dead thirty minutes ago."

Chapter 7

Not wanting to believe the nurse, Kayla quickly ran toward Mr. Jenson's room. He wasn't there, so she assumed that they had taken him down to the emergency unit to try to revive him. She ran through the main hall towards the elevator when she saw Raymond pacing back and forth with a look of agony on his face in the emergency waiting area. Mrs. Jenson was sitting down nervously shaking her leg trying to distract her thoughts with a magazine. The only thing Kayla couldn't figure out was *why was Bryan there*? He said that he and Erica weren't even close, but they were sitting beside one another holding hands like they were married. Distracted by her thoughts, Raymond finally looked up and slowly walked towards Kayla.

"I'm glad you're here," he said as he reached out his arms for a hug.

"I came down as soon as I heard. What's going on?" Kayla questioned, confused by their calmness.

"Well, dad had a light stroke and he had stop breathing for a few minutes. They have him breathing again, but they are running more tests to see if he is bleeding inside his head."

"Oh, Raymond, I'm so sorry," Kayla said, hugging him again.

"Who would've thought a night of partying would have brought this," Raymond sadly said.

"Well, what happened that night? Kayla discreetly asked as they walked up the hall away from the rest of the family.

"After you left, I told my mom to get out of the house. A few minutes later, dad, grabbed his keys and cut my hand in order to get me off of him. I left, but later I went back to the house after leaving your place. My mom told me dad fell. Do you think you could go and see if they have any updates?" He asked, quickly changing the subject.

"I could walk down and see, but there is no guarantee they will let me see him or tell me anything," Kayla softly responded.

"That's fine. Just knowing that he is still breathing is good enough for me."

Kayla agreed and headed towards the critical care unit. Kayla knew Raymond didn't believe a word of what his mom had told him and *why would Raymond say good enough for him, instead of good enough for us*, she thought. *Weren't they all concerned*? Kayla was good at interpreting body language and indirect vocabulary, so she knew something was being withheld in regards to what really happened that night.

Kayla snuck down to the critical care unit and instantly spotted Mr. Jenson. Doctors surrounded him and he appeared to be in a stable condition. She knew no one would tell her anything, but to her advantage, she recognized the head physician, who had two kids that attended the same daycare as Nicholas. She waited until he was away from the other doctors before deciding to approach him.

"Excuse me, Dr. Roberts," she called.

"Oh, hello Kayla, lovely to see you. How is Nicholas?"

"He is great, how are your kids?"

"Better than ever and working on another one," he joked.

"You are something else, Dr. Roberts," she flirtatiously commented. "Sir, Mr. Jenson is the father of a good friend of mine, and I was wondering could I give the family positive updates on his condition."

He deeply sighed, "Well, yes and no. Mr. Jenson is experiencing cerebral thrombosis, which caused him to have his stroke. His alcohol levels, at the time of the injury, were a huge factor in his condition.

"He's looking at major surgery then, right?"

"Well, that, or if we can't find the source of the clot in time, then there may not be any chances of saving him."

Sadness had overcome her. That was the last thing she wanted to tell Raymond.

"Hopefully, it'll be okay, Kayla," Dr. Roberts said as he gently rubbed Kayla's shoulder.

Just as he was walking off, Kayla asked, "Dr. Roberts is it normal that an injury like this could result from a slip and fall?"

He walked closer to her, looked around, and softly whispered. "Kayla, I've been in practice now for over twenty years and I've never seen results like this, on an adult, from just a slip and fall. This blow was projected by force, and not of that from a fall. You stay clear, be careful, and let the lawyers handle this," he warned as he walked off.

Dr. Roberts's words echoed in Kayla's head as she walked down the hall, ready to report to Raymond. Kayla had always suspected that something weird was going on according to the phone conversation she had had with Mrs. Jenson, and now Dr. Roberts had confirmed it. Someone in that house intended to hurt Mr. Jenson and Kayla suspected that everyone in that waiting room was hiding their involvement. Kayla slowly walked towards Raymond who was now sitting two seats away from his mom. As soon as he saw Kayla approaching, he quickly stood.

"I spoke with Dr. Roberts and he told me your dad was stable."

"That's great." Raymond sighed in relief. "Did he say anything else?"

"He also said that your father may need surgery," Kayla responded as the rest of the family spaciously gathered around her.

"Well, why do I get the feeling you're not telling me everything?" Raymond suspiciously asked.

"Raymond, when your father sustained the injury, his alcohol levels were off the roof, so this could have caused other complications besides the injury itself."

"What do you mean when he sustained the… injury?" Erica asked, standing there in defensive mode.

Kayla knew it wasn't time to have a confrontation with Erica. She gave her attention back to Raymond and addressed him directly.

"The doctor will be out here shortly in order to give you more detailed updates. Call me if you need me," she added, lightly touching his hand as she walked off.

Ending her shift, Kayla wondered whether or not she should go to her old workstation to see if she could get some updates on Destiny's condition. She didn't know whom to ask, especially since everyone knew that Destiny was the one who had gotten her transferred to another department. She thought that people would think she felt that Destiny deserved it. Instead, she decided to go home and get some decent rest since Nicholas would be at her mom's house for the next few days.

After arriving home and taking a long hot bath, Kayla decided to watch a movie and eat some left over spaghetti she had cooked the night before. She figured a funny movie or stand-up comedy show would ease her mind from the stressful situations at work. She finally flicked on the television and roamed through the channels until she found an old Ashton Kutcher movie she had never seen.

While watching the romantic comedy, Kayla started to feel alone and hopeless opposed to the spontaneously ambitious lovebirds in the movie. It took her back to the reality that she didn't have an official boyfriend or anyone to even cuddle with for the matter. She couldn't stop dwelling on the fact that she would have to meet someone new and start the dating process all over again with a stranger. She definitely didn't like the thought of introducing Nicholas to someone new as well.

Kayla went back to the refrigerator and grabbed a cold beer, thinking it would distract her mind off the romance and back into the comedy. The more she drank, the lonelier she felt. Kayla wanted someone to talk to, but she knew her options were limited. She could call Raymond, who had just betrayed her, or Michael, who had been a heartless dog the last few years. She picked up the phone and dialed a number.

"Hello," the voice answered.

"Hey," Kayla timidly spoke.

"Kayla? Is this you?" Michael asked.

"Uh, yes, I was calling to confirm our set up this weekend."

"Well, the last I checked we were still okay unless something between now and a few days ago changed."

"No, I was just making sure everything was still good, so I wouldn't have to make any sudden changes."

"There's nothing wrong with that accept for the fact that you decided to confirmed this in the wee hours of the morning," he joked.

"Yeah, well, I'm glad it's confirmed. Goodnight, Michael," Kayla sighed, about to hang up.

"No, wait, it isn't like that, baby. All I'm saying is that you don't have to have an excuse to call, sweetheart, I want to hear from you and Nicholas, too."

"Well, I didn't really want anything in particular. I was just relaxing watching a late show."

"Oh, okay. Where is little man, sleep?

"He's at my mom house for the rest of the week."

"Oh, you must be on call at the hospital this week?

"Yes, I have to make a lot of sacrifices in order for us to live comfortably, or at least until someone comes along and helps us out."

"What kind of help?"

"Well, I still hope to get married someday, Michael," she joked.

"Yeah, I feel you. I've been working a lot of overtime myself in order to get myself right," he stated, completely ignoring her last comment.

"Well, I guess that's great for you," she sarcastically replied.

"Look, I know I haven't been doing all what I'm supposed to do, but you know if you need something I got you."

"It's not that we're in need for something in particular, but anything that you give would help in the effort of raising our son."

"I know, Kayla, and I promise to do better. What about those lump sums you got when I filed my taxes? Did that help?"

"Michael, as long as I get assistance with Nicholas's daycare, the government keeps that money and probably vacations with it," she joked.

"Dang, I didn't know that."

"Well, now you know, so what time are you picking me up Saturday?" Kayla asked, quickly changing the subject.

"I was thinking around five, so we could have dinner and a movie, but I was going to ask what was wrong with hanging out tonight?"

"Tonight?" She questioned.

"Yeah, it would be like old times."

"Michael, I don't think that is a good idea."

"Why not?"

"First off, it's late and I wouldn't want you to get any false impressions in regards to coming over at this time."

Michael laughed hysterically, "Like what? Sex? Girl, I'm not trying to get in your pants, I just want to hang with you and catch up that's all. We do have a son together."

Kayla took a deep breath and finally agreed to let him come over. She got up from the bed and put on some silk pajamas then relocated in the living room. She needed to relax a little more, so she grabbed some vodka from the high cabinet and made herself a cocktail.

Thirty minutes later Michael showed up to Kayla's door wearing grey sweat pants and a plain Nike t-shirt. The truth of the matter was, Michael could have shown up in holey pants and a cut-off t-shirt and still would have been sexy in Kayla eyes.

As she opened the door, he had that boyish smile on his face as he reached in for a friendly hug. She offered him a drink, which he accepted as she made her way to the kitchen after escorting him into the living room. They sat on the couch and sipped their drinks as Kayla searched for a movie to watch. They began to make small talk during the movie about situations from their past relationship together while also discussing others they had both had been involved with since their breakup. After the movie was over and they had a few drinks in their system, Michael had grown quiet and stared blankly at the wall.

"Are you okay?" She asked.

"Did Nicholas ever call that Ray dude daddy?"

"No, he called him by his name."

"Did you tell him about me?"

"Of course, my son is and always will be aware of whom his real father is, but it's up to you to have a real relationship with him."

Michael again grew quiet and stared down at the floor as if he was searching for the right words. He held his head up and looked Kayla in her eyes as if he was hoping she had all the answers.

"What about you, Kayla, are you in love with him?"

"I'm…just…trying to figure myself out right now," she responded, trying to get her words together.

"Do you still love me?"

Kayla didn't know what to say as she stared back at him still shocked by the question. She had been waiting years for Michael to come back to rescue her and Nicholas, so they could be a family again.

After so much time had passed, Kayla's dreaming had just become a far-fetched hope turned non-existent. Although she still had love for Michael and her hormones were raging for passion, she couldn't feel any real sincerity or regret from Michael for abandoning them.

She refused to allow her emotions and sexual deprivation to distract her from seeing whether or not Michael was sincere about being prominent in Nicholas's life. Before getting herself involved, it was important for her to know if he was going to play dad or be a real father.

"Michael, look, it's beyond late and I don't feel this is the right time to have this type of conversation. There are still a lot of things that need to be addressed and I really don't want to mix my personal emotions in with what needs to be done for Nicholas. "

He sat there, stared at her for a minute, and shook his head in agreement. As he got up from the couch, he reached out his arms and embraced her with a passionate hug. She walked him to the door with her head down, lost in her thoughts. He slowly lifted her chin and gave her a slow, seductive kiss next to her lips.

"Goodnight, sweetheart," he whispered.

Chapter 8

The weekend had come and Michael hadn't held up his end
of the bargain once again. Kayla had attempted to contact him
through text and phone calls, but she didn't receive a response. She
wasn't sure if something had happened to him or if he was
deliberately standing her up. She figured the least he could have
done was have the decency to call and say he had a change of plans.
Although she was proud of herself for not letting her sexual desires
take control of her the other night, she was furious that she believed
Michael when he told her he was trying to do better by her and
Nicholas. Instead of sulking and reminding herself of what an idiot
she was as she normally would, Kayla went to the nearest liquor
store and decided to comfort herself with a bottle of Ciroc. She
didn't feel like being alone, so she decided to call her best friend,
Brandy, who she hadn't spoken to in a few months. She decided not
to bring up Michael's name or even mention the fact that they had
been in contact. She just wanted to forget her worries and hangout
for old time sake like they use to.

"Hey, Brandy, what's up?" Kayla asked, when Brandy answered the phone.

"Nothing much, girl, what are you up to?"

"I just went and got some Ciroc and I wanted to know did you want to have a few drinks?"

"Yeah, that's cool. I don't drink as much as I use to, but I'm down and I have a blunt, too."

After Kayla agreed to meet over at Brandy's crib, Kayla wasn't sure whether or not she wanted to start back smoking. She had a decent job and although Nicholas would be gone for the weekend, she hadn't smoked since he was born.

After arriving at Brandy's house, Kayla noticed that Brandy was already high and in the process of rolling another blunt as she walked behind her to the living area. She was still beautiful and nicely dressed in tan shorts and a flowing blouse that complimented her skin, but she looked rugged, as if she hadn't had any sleep in a few nights.

"What have you been up to?" Kayla asked breaking the ice.

"Nothing much. It has been a long time since we've had the time to really catch up, huh?"

"Yeah, seems like since I had Nicholas and been working at this hospital, all I have had time for is him and work."

"I feel you, girl. I just got laid off about three months ago from a hellhole factory and I'm not messed up about it," Brandy laughed. "So what's going, has Michael been to see Nicholas yet?"

"Girl, he saw him a few times, but nothing steady." Kayla didn't feel like getting into details, so she kept it vague.

"Oh, okay. You know my son's dad not shit either, so I definitely understand."

Changing the subject, Kayla had begun to tell Brandy about what happened between her and her co-worker, Destiny. Brandy agreed that there was something about Destiny's alleged rape that didn't sound right. In the midst of smoking and drinking, they continued to catch up on situations in their lives, and an hour later, they were laughing their heads off from being intoxicated.

"Let's go out tonight, I haven't been to a club in a while," Brandy offered.

"I don't know, girl, but I really don't do clubs."

"Aw, come on, girl, it's a nice sophisticated club where you have to dress to impress, no tennis shoes or hats."

"I guess. Let me drink some more of this vodka so I can see how I feel in about an hour."

Brandy had gotten up from the couch and grabbed a pill bottle from the top counter. "Here, take one of these."

"What is this?" Kayla asked.

"Girl, it's a hydro. You've never taken a hydro before?"

"Uh, no." Kayla hesitantly responded while grabbing it.

"It's cool, it makes you relax and I promise you won't even be worried about any of that bullshit you have going on in your life right now." Brandy laughed.

After leaving Brandy's house, Kayla had agreed to go home and change in order to go to the "sophisticated" club that Brandy mentioned.

Once at home, she rummaged through her closet and grabbed a sleek, form-fitting black dress and her suede booties to match. She pinned her hair up, threw on some silver accessories, and she deemed herself ready for a night out on the town. Before walking out of the door, her phone rang.

"Hey, Kayla, this is Michael."

"Oh, what's up," she responded in an irritated tone.

"Look, I know you're mad and I know I promised you a date, but some things came up and I just couldn't make it."

"So you decided to call me at 10:30 tonight to tell me this."

"You don't have to have an attitude, Kayla, I said I was sorry and I'm calling now to let you know I want to make it up to you."

"Gee, that sounds familiar. Look Michael, I am walking out the door as we speak. Brandy and I are about to go clubbin' so I guess I'll see you some other time."

"What club are yall going to?"

"I'm not sure. Some sophisticated club that requires you to dress up, so I'll talk to you later," she added as she rushed off the phone.

She decided that she wasn't going to allow Michael or anyone else to ruin her night. It had been a long time since she had been out and she was feeling good from drugs.

After entering the club, Brandy and Kayla went to the bar for more drinks in to keep their momentum going. They walked around and mingled with a few common associates as they approached the dance floor.

After being on the floor for a few songs, Kayla felt a firm hand tap her on her shoulder. She turned only to see Bryan smiling at her like a Cheshire cat.

"Hey, beautiful, I see your doing your thing tonight."

"Hello, Bryan, how are you?" she asked, giving him a tight hug.

"I'm not use to seeing you out here, this must be your first time out?" he questioned.

"Something like that. So where is your right hand man, Erica?"

"Look, let's get this straight, Erica is not my woman. Besides, she would be more into you then she would me."

"Whatever," Kayla said, brushing him off.

"Hey, but check this, seriously, when are you going to allow me to take you out?"

"Honestly, I'm not into players, Bryan, I have a son."

"What have I done to indicate to you that I'm a player?"

"You come to the club all of the time, right?"

"So…do you think if I had a woman I would be here? What else is there to do when you're single?"

"Look, I just broke up with Raymond. How would it look if I all of the sudden started dating his sister's 'friend' and I use that term loosely."

"It would look like we two grown ass people doing what we want to do. It's not my fault he was a jackass. Why should I be withheld from something that might turn out to be great?"

All Kayla could do was smile. He was charming and sexy as hell. "Maybe we could get to know one another and see where it goes. Here's my number." Kayla offered, reaching into his pocket and grabbing his cell phone. She had totally forgotten he already had her number, but her actions still turned him on.

"I'll text you." He smiled as he walked away.

"Okay, you go girl!" Brandy said as Bryan walked out of sight.

"Girl, it's nothing, just someone to talk to from time to time."

The club was over, so Kayla headed back home after a great night out. She still felt relaxed, although, some of her intoxication had decreased. When she had pulled up to her street, she noticed a car parked in front of her home. It was Raymond waiting outside. *Why the hell is Raymond in my driveway unannounced?* She thought. *Were Raymond and Bryan trying to play some type of sick joke on me? He has the nerve, what if I had had company.* She wasn't sure what she would do or if she would even get out of the car as she pulled up in her driveway. She remembered the last episode she encountered when Raymond was at her house, so she didn't know what to expect. Raymond stepped out of his car and walked to her door as Kayla cracked the window giving him only enough room to talk.

"It's like that, Kayla?"

"Well, Raymond it is 2 in the morning and you are sitting outside of my house uninvited, so what do you expect."

"I mean, I called. I'm sorry, Kayla, I just needed someone to talk to right now. I'm sorry about all the bad things I've done to you.

You're a good woman and I took advantage of the great relationship we had."

"Everyone makes mistakes, Raymond; it's what we do after the mistake that counts."

"Yeah, well, my dad just went into a coma and the doctor's not sure if he is going to make it," he said as tears welled in his eyes.

"I'm so sorry to hear that, Raymond. No one even told me."

"It just happened about four hours ago. My mom and sister, along with a few other family members, are still there."

Kayla was still reluctant to roll down the window due to his emotional state. Anything could set him off. There was a long awkward moment of silence as she listened to Raymond sniffle a few times.

"Well, if there is anything I can do to help just let me know."

"You can start by rolling this damn window down and quit treating me like an ex-fucking convict," he sternly demanded.

"Raymond, you are a little emotional right now, I really don't think that's a good idea if…"

"DAMN YOU!" he abruptly yelled and hit the driver window and walked off. He got into his car a sped off. Kayla made sure that Raymond was far up the street before she ran in the house. *Raymond was turning into a maniac* she thought as she locked the bolts on the door and turned on her cell phone. She had four missed calls, one from Michael and three earlier from Raymond. Just as she set the phone down to get undressed; she received a text message from Bryan.

Bryan: Did you make it home okay?

Kayla: Yes, thanks

Bryan: Good, just saying goodnight...ttyl

Kayla didn't want to be home alone, so she decided to call Michael to see if he would come over. He answered the phone and she briefly explained what was going on. Michael had no problem coming to her rescue. He arrived about fifteen minutes later in combat mode as she opened the door and let him in the house.

"Where the fuck this nigga at, mane?" He firmly questioned.

"Calm down, Michael, he already left. Let's go in my room so we can watch television or something."

She led him to her room and told him to have a seat on the bed as she sat down next to him.

"I guess he was afraid that his dad may die so he didn't know how to control his aggression."

"I don't give a damn. Don't nobody suppose to wait at your house and start banging on windows and shit. What if Nicholas had been in the car with you? Call him tell him to come back over."

"Michael, please. You ending up in jail isn't going to help my situation. Let's just chill and relax, okay?" she softly pleaded.

Still fired up, Kayla had to calm Michael down with a few jokes as she got up and put on some soft music.

"So, how are you going to make up missing our date," Kayla asked, switching the subject.

"I don't know, what do you want me to do?"

"I don't know. I guess you could massage my back. That is, if you still know how." She teased.

He scooted back, sat her down between his legs, and began to massage her back.

"Are you serious? Are you really trying to massage me through a shirt?"

"I don't need instructions. I got this." He complained.

"It has been a while so…sometimes things need a refreshing." She teased.

"I could never get rusty when it comes to you, sweetheart."

After a minute or two, he slowly lifted her shirt as he pressed his hands firmly against her skin moving his hands toward her upper shoulders. He slid his hands slowly down her back above her buttocks and gently squeezed while simultaneously moving his thumbs in circular motions. Kayla felt every inch of her body tense as her hormones anticipated the intimacy. She needed to be touched. She needed to be caressed. She needed every inch of his manhood rotating and sliding in and out of her vagina. He must have felt her intensity because he made a bold move by sliding his hands toward her chest as he cupped her breast in his hands and softly began kissing her on the neck.

Kayla couldn't resist as she grabbed his hand and move it down to her wetness. She moaned in pleasure as he massaged her clitoris and moved his fingers in and out her wetness while passionately kissing her around the ear. She stood up; he slowly removed her clothes as he shook his head in admiration of her body.

She watched him hungrily as he grabbed protection from his right pocket and placed it on his stiffness.

She walked over to the door to reassure herself that it was still locked, and then turned off the lights. He lied back as she got on top of him and carefully placed him inside of her. She moved back and forth in harmony with his rotation. He balanced her breast in his hands as she squeezed his hands and told him to push his dick harder inside her wetness. She licked her lips and moaned as he instantly followed her instructions. While leaving his left hand on her breast, he took his right hand and slapped her booty cheek then firmly held on to it. It drove her wild and she sped up her momentum as well. Kayla could feel her pleasure about to come down and he must have too because his upward thrust was firmer and deeper. Kayla released a soft sigh of ecstasy as they climaxed together. Kayla fell asleep in her temporary moment of sexual glory.

Chapter 9

After Michael left the following Sunday afternoon, Kayla couldn't believe what she had done. It definitely wasn't her intentions to have slept with Michael again, but the drugs and sexual needs definitely made her lower her standards. The last thing that she wanted to do was to get herself psyched for a family she may never have. Although he had told her in the mist of their sexual escapade that he loved her, she didn't want to set herself up for disappointment. She was determined not to let it interfere with what she had going on, but she couldn't help the fact that she had rekindled some of her old feelings. She wasn't sure what to expect because Michael and she hadn't talk about what would happen next. She decided not to assume anything and treat Michael just as her child's father while continuing to befriend Bryan.

A few hours later, Kayla had brought Nicholas home and decided to prepare his favorite dish of fried chicken, mash potatoes with gravy, and cornbread. As she was finishing up, she received a phone call from an unknown number. She assumed that it was Michael since he hadn't call since he left earlier.

"Hello, is this Kayla?" the strange older female voiced asked.

"Uh, yes, but who is this?"

"You don't know me, but I'm Dana's mom."

Kayla's heart dropped. "Oh, uh, okay."

"I'm sorry to bother you, but I had a few questions for you if you don't mind."

"Well, I'm just getting ready for dinner, so now is really not a good time, I'm sorry-"

"Just a few minutes please," the older lady interrupted, "Did you know of anyone my daughter was dating around the time of her death?"

"Uh, not in particular, she vaguely mentioned a few guys I guess."

"Do you remember any names?"

"Look, Dana's mom, I'm sorry for your lost, but why do you feel the need to investigate me and how did you get my number?"

"How would you feel if you lost your child?" she began to cry. "My daughter was pregnant and there is no way in this world some cops are going to tell me my daughter committed suicide."

"I wish I could help you ma'am but I just can't."

"Well, tell me who Mr. Goodbar is?" she forced.

Kayla quickly hung up.

The situation threw off her entire train of thought. The name Mr. Goodbar did not ring a bell, but anything surrounding Dana's death and George caused immediate fear. She wasn't sure if she should go somewhere and hide for a while or find a new place to stay altogether. George, in her eyes was a real-life killer, something that only happened on television in her world. She knew people killed, but she never thought it would be someone she had lived with. With Raymond going crazy, Michael giving mixed signals again, and the new developing investigation surrounding Dana's death, Kayla felt backed into a corner. It was entirely too much to deal with at once.

Later on that day, Kayla needed to get away from it all and put herself in a different setting. She called Bryan, who agreed to meet up with her to grab a bite to eat. Kayla didn't want the outing to seem like a romantic gesture so she dressed down in jeans, t-shirt, and tennis shoes. Furthermore, when she arrived at the restaurant she sat in the bar area at a high top table that was positioned so she could see everyone who walked through the door. Bryan arrived about ten minutes later wearing khaki pants, a light blue polo vest that covered his ivory under shirt, and dark printed alligator loafers. Kayla motioned him to where she was sitting and he walked over giving her a nice seductive smile as he sat down in front of her.

"You look nice, I was under the impression this was a causal outing," Kayla said.

"It's all good, this is my normal attire. I didn't even consider the fact that I would be sitting here with a beautiful woman," he teased.

For some reason, Bryan's perfect response to almost everything became slightly bothersome. He didn't seem real to her at times, because everything he said seemed pre-calculated.

"So, you finally decided to take a chance on greatness," he said, disrupting her thoughts.

"Huh? You're not really that shallow are you?" She asked, suddenly repulsed.

"No," he laughed, "You took that the wrong way. I was thinking about the possibility of you and me dating."

"Uh, well, I am thinking more of a friendship, Bryan, dating exclusively is not in my path right now."

"Why not," he asked, disappointed by her rejection.

"Didn't we kind of discuss this already? You are too close for comfort with my ex's family."

"If that's the case, why are we having lunch?"

"We both eat don't we, Bryan? That doesn't have anything do with a relationship."

"Look, Raymond shouldn't be a reason not to date me or anyone else. It's not my fault that the real boy doesn't recognize talent when he sees it."

"Talent?"

"Yes, talent or in other words, natural born greatness."

"You know, Bryan, your choice of words sometimes makes me wonder is this actually you or do you just say things because they sound good?"

"That's a slick insult, but perhaps a fair question, I guess.

First off, you shouldn't judge a man by his words, but by his actions."

"That's true, but a man has to be a man of his word and the actions to follow are a mere justification of those words."

"Do you always have to have the last words or win every discussion?" He asked, aggravated by her wittiness.

"No, but to my defense, have you ever thought that you, like most men, feel intimidated by an intellectually independent woman?" She challenged.

He sat back in his seat and stared coldly as if he wanted to defy her statement. He looked down and shook his head, because he knew he wouldn't get anywhere by continuing the argument.

"Look, all I know is that since the first day I saw you, you've kept me curious to know more about you on a personal level. It's something about the look in your eyes that keeps me intrigued."

With that comment, the entire mood had softened and they began to gradually learn more about one another. Bryan was an only child raised solely by his mom. He quit college and started working full-time for Mr. Jenson's landscaping company, which helped explain his personal connection with the Jensons. He said he had every intention to return to school, but he needed to help his mom, who has a condition he cared not to discuss. Talking with Bryan made Kayla realize he wasn't a conceited jerk after all.

He seemed ambitious and genuine, especially when he spoke of his mother, but overall he also seemed to have a great deal of respect for women in general, even when he referred to ex-girlfriends.

After finishing their meal, Bryan paid for the food and escorted Kayla to her car. For some strange reason, she wanted to rush up to him and give him a tight hug, but she withheld the urges inside.

"I had a good time getting to know you and if it's okay, I would love to talk to and see you again." He stated.

"That sound nice," she smiled, "I think I would like that, too."

"Do you think or do you know," He teased, grabbing her hand.

"I know," she blushed.

As he walked back towards his car, he turned around as if he had forgotten something. Kayla thought he might have been coming back for a kiss. At that point, she would have accepted a peck or two on the jaw.

"Hey, uh, Kayla does Mr. Jenson remember anything about that night?"

"I'm not sure, he hasn't really been stable, and why do you ask?

"No reason, Erica had just been nagging me like I'm suppose to know more than the family knows since I work for him, you know? He explained himself as if he needed confirmation that Kayla believed him. She nodded her head in agreement then he walked off leaving behind a handsome smile. Bryan's curiosity infused Kayla's curiosity. Kayla wondered, *why Erica would question Bryan when he wasn't even there at the time of the incident. On the other hand, was he?*

Chapter 10

It was now the end of September, three months after Kayla's outing with Bryan and things were looking up for Kayla. She received her promotion to shift leader at the hospital in addition to working only two weekends a month. There was still no communication from Michael, but she did receive her first child support check three weeks prior. Furthermore, Bryan and Kayla had become extremely close over the last few months. He helped pay the deductible on her damaged car door because he didn't want Kayla to have any future dealings with Raymond's erratic behavior. He also had opened up to Kayla in regards to his mom's pill addiction. Little did he know that Kayla had gained a small addiction as well. Since the night Brandy had given her a hydro, Kayla found herself to be more sociable and relaxed around co-workers, family, and friends whenever she took one, so Brandy and her had began to jointly purchase pill packages from a street distributor. She couldn't tell Bryan because she knew how much he hated his mother's addiction.

However, she did tell him the truth about George and his association with Dana's death. For some reason, Kayla felt that Bryan might have felt it was his obligation to protect her from all the bad men in her life. She still hadn't introduced him to Nicholas who still questioned the return of his dad, but if all went well she decided she would introduce them based upon Bryan's many requests.

As Kayla was sitting at home one Sunday afternoon watching television, she reminisced as she watched Nicholas play with his motorcycle. It ate her up inside how she allowed Michael back into their lives only to disappoint them both. What made it worse was when Nicholas would ask when was his dad coming back to see him. Kayla's only response was on dad's time. One day Nicholas went further and asked why dad's time can't be all the time? She had to tell him that dad's priorities weren't together and Nicholas acted as if he understood, because he never asked again. The only meager satisfaction in Kayla's eyes was that Nicholas would learn at an early age that his mother wasn't the blame for his dad's absence.

Deciding not to further sulk about the situation, Kayla reached from the couch to her end table and grabbed a traveling brochure she gotten in the mail a few weeks earlier. Kayla thought it would be nice to have a change of scenery, but when would she have the time to take off and where would she go? Furthermore, she didn't want to leave her baby boy for an entire week. She finally decided in her mind that she needed the time to relax and have time for her. She still wasn't sure exactly where she was going, all she knew was that she wanted to go.

Towards the end of her work week, Kayla was slightly apprehensive about putting in a vacation when she recently got a promotion. She had decided to wait towards the end of her shift when things around the hospital would be calm. Kayla had mentally prepared herself just in case her supervisor denied her request; however, her senior supervisor who always boasted about Kayla's hard work readily approved it.

Later that night, when Kayla left work and was about to call Bryan to tell him the good news, out of her peripheral vision, she could see someone on crutches approaching her.

"Kayla, can we talk for a minute?"

She turned to see a bruised up Destiny with a cast on her leg, in addition to a few bandages. Destiny stood there as if she was waiting on some type of sympathy hug or comfort, but Kayla wasn't interested. Even though she never wished any type of brutality on women, she still wasn't fond enough of Destiny to offer any type of compassion. She still hadn't forgotten about the rumors either. She heard that Destiny banged herself up in order to get the married man that she was sleeping with in jail.

"What do you want to talk about?" Kayla asked dryly, interrupting the silence.

"I just wanted to come over and say congratulations on your promotion," Destiny gleefully responded, noticing Kayla's cold shoulder.

"Yeah, thanks, well good luck with everything," Kayla hurriedly stated, walking off.

"Wait Kayla, I know your not that fucking heartless are you? You see me here barely standing on one leg."

As much as Kayla wanted to turn back around and give her a piece of her mind, she continued to walk because she didn't want to be twisted into any more drama.

"I gave my lawyer your name and number as a witness!" Destiny yelled.

Kayla slowly turned around in disbelief of what she just heard. She knew this chick had to be mentally disturbed.

"You did what?" Kayla asked, angrily approaching her.

"Well, my lawyer asked me did I discuss my relationship with anyone and I told him YOU were my confidant." She cheered.

"Look, Destiny, it's unfortunate what 'may' have happened to you, but I have nothing to do with your personal life."

"Of course you do Miss Advice Giver," she wickedly smiled, "so if you don't testify on my behalf, I will tell the court that you encourage me to continue to see Mike. Destiny wins again," she chanted as she limped down the hall.

Kayla stood there with a bewildered looked on her face. She thought to herself, *this bitch has lost her mind to think that I would do anything for her*. Kayla knew that if she allowed Destiny's lawyer to trick her into appearing in court, the girl she gave the note to at the restaurant could possibly be there and identify her, making her an accessory to the crime. The thought alone frighten her and going to jail wasn't an option. Kayla knew she was willing to do whatever it took to disassociate her from anything that had to do with Destiny.

It was hard for her to hate people, but she really had built an enormous amount of disgust even at the thought of Destiny Walker.

Once in the car, Kayla immediately called Bryan to talk to him about the threat from Destiny, but he didn't answer. She called again, still no answer. She waited until she pulled up into her driveway to try back, but this time, someone picked up and she heard a woman yelling hysterically in the background, and then the phone went dead.

Kayla took a deep breath as she held the phone in her hand confused by what she just heard. At first thought, she assumed it may have been his mom, but she heard Bryan talk to his mom on several occasions, so she couldn't imagine something between them getting that escalated. She sat in the car thinking of the call and decided that it was best to cut Bryan off completely. Although they have never had sex and were not an established couple, she didn't have the time nor energy to deal with extra drama from other women. She felt that since she wasn't having sex with Bryan, he was probably getting it from the hysterical woman, so she couldn't and refused to compete. The even bigger truth of the matter was that she had become too dependant on his companionship, so she needed to break loose before her feelings got stronger than they already were.

About an hour later, Kayla had just settled into bed when Bryan returned her call. She decided to ignore his call and speak to him the next day in regards to her decision, but he was persistent. He called back to back, which he had never done before, so Kayla picked up, thinking it just might be an emergency.

"Hello, Bryan? Are you okay?"

"Am I okay? What took you so long to answer?" He asked, highly frustrated.

"I was in the bed, so I figured everything could wait until tomorrow."

"Kayla, nothing has ever waited until tomorrow, so what is the real problem?"

"I was calling you earlier to talk about the Destiny situation and how the bitch calls herself threatening me, but I was thrown off by some woman screaming at the top of her lungs at you once you finally picked your phone up."

"Oh, well, what did she say?" He asked.

"You should know, Bryan, she was screaming at you."

"I was talking about what did Destiny say?"

"Oh, so you decided to ignore the fact that I heard you arguing with some woman?"

"I heard what you asked I just chose not to address it."

"What do you mean you chose not to address it, we talk about everything when it comes to me, but there are limits with you?"

"No, let's get this straight right now. You set the limits months ago when you decided just to be friends," he sternly argued, "and now you want to dip into my personal life since you don't have one."

The moment had gotten so quiet it became uncomfortable.

"You know what, Bryan, you don't know shit about me, and so there is no need in us being friends or anything else. Have a good life."

"Kayla, wait. Are you really about to end what we have over something this petty."

"Bryan, you made it very clear that my no-life-having-ass is banned from your glorious personal life."

"Kayla, what do you want from me? I asked you months ago to date exclusively and you said no, but I was willing to accept your friendship because you seemed to be someone I wanted constantly in my life."

"And this is why I said no, Bryan, because had we been in a relationship, this would have been a huge problem."

"Kayla, we are not even in a relationship now and it's already a huge problem."

"I know," she sighed, "which is why I feel we need a break. I am getting extremely attached to you and I feel like I am the only one who has the potential of getting hurt."

There was another awkward silence until Bryan finally said okay and hung up his phone. Kayla then lied down thinking how grateful she was for never letting Bryan get too close to her heart nor her panties. He was a self-serving opportunist who only looked out for his best interest. Kayla closed her eyes as a tear rolled down her face. As quick as the friendship had started, it had ended even sooner.

A few weeks had passed, it was the weekend and Kayla was spending extra quality time with her son since she was leaving soon for her vacation. She was convinced to go on a cruise with Gabby and Gabby's husband, who had an uncle who was the general manager of a few cruise lines.

They were all able to get unbelievable rates on a five-day four-night stay. Kayla wasn't exactly thrilled about going solo and being a third wheel, but at least she would have someone there she knew.

Later that Saturday night once Nicholas was cozy in bed asleep, Kayla decided to invite Brandy over for a few drinks and split their normal round of pills they had purchased from "the guy" each month. Kayla called him "the guy" because Brandy was discrete in regards to their supplier. She thought Brandy might have been slick dating him.

Once at the house, Brandy and Kayla engaged in their routine gossip and popped off a few rounds of pills and drinks as usual. Brandy was in the process of telling Kayla how a mutual associate of theirs requested that Brandy engage in a threesome when Kayla's phone rang.

"Girl, let me hurry and lose whoever this is on this phone, because I have to hear this!" Kayla exclaimed. Not exactly recognizing the number, Kayla hurriedly said hello.

"You lowdown bitch," said the angry male voice.

"Who the fuck is this?" Kayla countered.

"You know who this is and you paying for my brand new set of tires, cunt."

"Now that I hear your weak ass voice I know it's Raymond, but don't you ever call my phone again disrespecting me, you male whore."

"Bitch, I will come over there right now and choke you until you turn blue."

"Look here, you dumb freak show, don't be accusing me of bullshit one of your other freaks did," Kayla lied, "and by the time you get here, the police, along with my new boo will be waiting on you with their guns, faggot."

"Fuck you and your weak ass boyfriend; I'm Raymond and you paying for my car."

"Keep your hoes in line and lose my number punk."

"My neighbor said that she seen you sneaking around late at night a few months back around the same time my tires had gotten slashed."

"You so dam dumb. How somebody gone remember some shit that happened damn near five months ago around the time we were dating. Boy, kill yo'self."

"You just a loser ass jump off, with a kid, I shouldn't have ever gave you the time of day."

"Raymond, you shouldn't be worried about me. What you should be worried about is your dad's life-threatening head injuries and how your mom is fucking kids." Kayla knew she went overboard, but she didn't care. She was sick of him judging her for having a kid. Their was a brief moment of silence.

"You dead, bitch." Raymond threatened, as he hung up.

"Girl, you okay? What was that about?" Brandy asked.

"Girl, I'm cool, you know how these men get upset once you move on."

"Yeah, but I know how they can get crazy too. Do you want me to spend a night?"

"Girl I'm fine, finish telling me the story."

"Are you sure, because I will cut up?"

"I'm good, girl, thanks, now finish."

Although Kayla and Brandy continued to talk another hour and a half, Kayla was still stirred up inside. She knew that it was a big possibility he had drove by to see if Kayla was bluffing or not.

She didn't want to stall Brandy or make it seem like she was scared, so she decided to set her pride aside and go in the bathroom so she could call Bryan. If he didn't answer, Kayla decided she would pack up Nicholas and go over to her mom's house for the night. The more she thought about how Raymond continued to act like a fool, the more upset she got. By the time Bryan answered the phone, she was hysterical.

"Hello," He answered.

"Bryan, I need help."

"Kayla, what's wrong, what happened?"

"I need a gun, right now!" she exclaimed.

"Wait, what's going on Kayla?

"I will not continue to be threatened in my own home with my son, I need a gun now!"

"Calm down, I'm on my way."

After drying her face and calming down, she went back into the living room where Brandy was packing up her things about to leave. She, again, asked Kayla if she was okay and, again, Kayla insured her that everything was good. As soon as Brandy walked out the door, Kayla ran back in the living room, popped two hydros, then put them in a stash spot.

She was hoping Bryan would show before Raymond, but much to her disappointment, he did not. A few minutes after Brandy had drove off, Raymond promptly pulled up. He apparently had been waiting somewhere close, waiting on his opportunity to strike.

"Come on, bitch, let's get this done. You had huge balls on the phone," he yelled, while banging on the door.

"The police are on the way right now you maniac and you better hope my son doesn't wake up." Kayla yelled back.

"I don't give a damn. We don't care about families and shit. Remember what you just said about my folks."

Just as Kayla was dialing the phone, a set of headlights flashed through her front room blinds. She knew it was Bryan coming to her rescue and at that moment, she could have literally proposed to him.

She looked out the window and watched how Raymond uncomfortably stepped down from her porch. Blinded by the lights, Raymond must have thought it was the police because he shamefully held his head down and slowly walked toward the car with his hands in his pockets. Kayla opened the door and stood motionless in front of it still holding the knob. Bryan got out the car and calmly, but promptly approached Raymond.

"Are you fucking kidding me?" Raymond angrily laughed.

"You of all people fucking my bitch."

"First off, you need to lower your voice and refrain from the name calling because there ain't any bitches around here."

"Is this a joke? Are you trying to roll up on me? Weak ass Bryan trying to roll up on Raymond." He teased, as he challengingly stepped closer to Bryan.

"Look, Raymond, you smell like you have been drinking and you need to leave while you're ahead and once you leave, I need you to pretend like this house is a foreign country that you haven't heard of."

"You a little bitch," Raymond said as he suddenly pushed Bryan who stumbled back almost losing his balance.

"Raymond, I'm warning you, dog."

"I thought there weren't any bitches around here," Raymond, mocked as he pushed him again. Bryan had had enough. He slightly turned as if he was about to walk away but swiftly threw Raymond a right hook to the jaw that promptly knocked him to the ground. Bryan hovered over Raymond, waiting on him to get up so he could strike again.

"Now, who's the bitch, punk," he tormented, as he kicked Raymond in the torso. He continued to preach as he kicked him again. Kayla, now afraid of what Bryan may do, walked over to the end of her porch steps and firmly called Bryan's name. He looked up as if he had forgotten where he was. He slowly stepped back and told Raymond not to ever come back. Once Bryan had gotten to where Kayla stood, Raymond got up and limped back towards the car swearing and yelling at both of them. As Bryan watched Raymond slowly drive off, Kayla softly grabbed his hand and walked him in the house. He followed her to the living room and told him to wait while she checked to see if Nicholas had awakened. Still sound asleep, she grabbed another pill from her stash, chewed it, then returned to Bryan who looked as if he was saying a prayer.

"Are you okay?" she asked.

"You're kidding, right? Once Mrs. Jenson finds out I kicked her son's ass, I'm good as fired."

"Maybe if you talked to her first then-"

"No, Kayla. I can't talk to the mother of the son I just beat." He angrily vented.

"Well, for what it's worth, I thank you. Lord only knows what he would have tried had you not showed up."

He took a deep breath, shook his head, and then looked her in the eyes. *God he is handsome* she thought.

"I'm sorry…you're right. I am glad you called. Are you okay?"

She nodded.

"Well, if it's okay. I wouldn't mind staying a little while longer to make sure he doesn't come back."

"I was hoping you'd say that," she smiled feeling relaxed from the medication, "I just can't wait to go on this cruise and get away from it all."

"Cruise?" He questioned.

"Yeah, my supervisor hooked me up."

"So, it's just you two going?"

"No, she is bringing her husband, so it is kind of a third wheel situation."

"Oh, sounds fun, I guess," he said, sounding a tad bit condescending.

"What do you mean, *you guess*?"

"Kayla, if we were as close as I thought we were, why didn't I know or why wasn't I invited on this cruise?"

"Perhaps, because I was under the impression our friendship was over."

"Really, Kayla, you know that's a lie, because if you thought that, you wouldn't have called me tonight. You were doing what most women do; you were waiting to see if I would call you first."

"If that's the case, I sure did lose," she said with sarcasm.

"It doesn't matter who calls first. As long as you know I'm here for you and Nicholas that's all that matters and I feel like I proved that to you tonight."

"I know now, but you have to give me a break, Bryan, this is the first time a situation like this has ever occurred in our friendship."

"You mean, in our relationship." He corrected.

She sighed. "Listen, Bryan, relationships are serious. I don't date to date, I date to marry."

"Don't you think I know this, Kayla? Don't you think I would have left you alone a long time ago if I didn't want to be serious?"

"Not necessarily, it may just be I'm a challenge."

"A challenged?" he laughed, "you of all people should know that I have one challenge right now and that's to get my mom off pills, well, maybe two challenges, but I sincerely care for you and I want you to be my woman."

He was so fine and his directness turned Kayla on to a point where she wanted to pounce him, but she knew it wasn't the time.

"So, where do we go from here," she asked, suppressing her sexual desires.

"First off," he said as he got up, sat next her, and put his arms around her, "you never go this long without talking to me again. From there, we take it slow and everything else will fall in place." *He seems so warm and sincere* she thought. She wondered if she should ask him to go on the cruise since they were now an official couple.

For the most part, she wasn't sure if she was ready to go through the stages of opening up her mind, body, and soul to him or any man. She knew eventually she would get involved again, so why not start with someone she had a little history with and comfortable around.

"So, do you think your boss or whoever's covering for Mr. Jenson would let you off on a short notice?"

"Uh…I don't know," he answered, seemingly uncomfortable with the questioned at hand.

"Who's running the business while Mr. Jenson is at the Recovery Clinic?"

"The Recovery Clinic?" He asked, sounding shocked.

"That's where they told the hospital he had been moved to."

He sat there for a minute and awkwardly looked at her. He then put his head into his hands and shook his head. He must have thought what she said was ridiculous.

"I'll see if I can get off, provided I still have my job, okay?"

"Okay…so what's the secret? Is there something wrong with the story or what?

"Are you asking me because you're curious or because you want to go report to Raymond?"

"Mr. Jenson was our patient, Bryan, so yes; my staff and I would like to know how he is doing."

"You're right, I'm sorry. The last I heard he was in a nursing home recovering."

"That's good to hear, because for a minute, the doctor had said they couldn't get the bleeding to stop."

"It's getting late so I guess I'll head out and call you two in the morning, okay?"

He stood up, grabbed Kayla's hand, and walked towards the door. He gave her a gentle kiss above her top lip and then directly on the lips as he walked out the door. She watched him as he got in the car and drove away. He made her feel special and so adored that she was beginning to feel more confident about their new relationship. There was this one issue, however, she wasn't sure if Bryan was jealous of Raymond or if there was some other reason he was so sensitive whenever they spoke about the Jensons.

Chapter 11

It was finally vacation day for Kayla and Bryan and they were ready to take their flight out to Florida so they could meet at the dock of the cruise ship. Their new relationship appeared to be flawless. Kayla had finally introduced Bryan and Nicholas who were hitting it off quite well. In his free time, Bryan took Nicholas practically everywhere he went, bought him toys, and taught him how to do boy things. Although it was too soon to move in together, Bryan occasionally stayed overnight, helped with fixes, cleaning, and cooking around the house. As good as things were going, they still hadn't explored the sexual aspect of their relationship. Kayla figured that the alone time they would have on the trip would be the perfect time to engage in grown up activity. They left Kayla's car at home and drove Bryan's car so it would appear that they weren't on vacation. Bryan still stayed in an apartment complex, so he was fine with the idea. After giving Nicholas at least a thousand kisses, she left him at her mother's house and headed to the airport.

Sitting in the waiting area, Kayla could feel her body tense up as it was nearing time for their flight. She knew that she might not be able to get over her first time flying fears, so she brought her comfort pills that she upgraded to a higher dosage and milligram. She continued to hide her habit from Bryan because he and his mom hadn't been speaking since his mom promised she would rehab but reneged on the deal. Kayla figured she had become his only confidant without the association with his mother since Bryan and his mother were extremely close. She knew he was hurting inside and for him to find out his woman was addicted as well would only add insult to injury. She attempted to get him to call his mom on several occasion, but Bryan was extremely stubborn and adamant regarding his position.

There were five minutes until boarding time and Kayla was literally shaking from the thoughts of being on an airplane. Bryan held her hand while whispering comforting thoughts and plans in her ear. If anything, the whispering turned her on but definitely didn't relax her. Kayla eased to the restroom to do what she felt was best, she popped three pills. Twenty minutes later Kayla was on the plane feeling a little calmer and excited as she sat in the window seat next to Bryan. He softly stroked her hand as she began to think about how much she missed Nicholas already. She hadn't been this far away from him since he was born. She took a deep breath, sat back, relaxed, and closed her eyes as she fantasized about making love to Bryan for the first time.

She wondered if he would take his time, tease her, and caress her in every place that yearn for attention or would he be one of those "I haven't done it in while, sorry I came so fast" type of guys. The more she thought about it, Bryan hadn't tried to make a sexual advance towards her at all. He made a few comments, but it was only when she brought up the subject. She figured it had to be one of three things; he was one of the most respectful men in the world, he already had a chick he was banging, or last but hopefully the least, he was gay. Either way the mystery of Bryan would soon be revealed.

Safely off the plane, the two of them had taken a shuttle to the loading dock where the ship awaited. Walking hand and hand across the boardwalk and up the stairs, Kayla looked upon the massive ship in awe. She felt like a kid in a candy store as she walked across the deck marveled by the open view of the onboard water park. The greetings from the crewmembers were gracious as they walked around serving wine and hors d'oeuvres. After a short meet and greet, the two walked toward the double glass doors to find their room so they could unwind before the night's festivities. Glancing across the poolside on the way to find their room, Kayla paused as she suddenly felt her heart race twice the normal speed. Noticing her hesitation, Bryan asked what was wrong as he encouraged her to continue walking with a gentle tug of her hand. She said it was nothing as she quickly looked back toward the other side of the pool where she thought she saw Jessica, George's wife.

Once in the room, they pulled backed the curtains on the glass doors and invited in the sunlight, giving the room the perfect touch of elegancy along with the flowers and welcome note on the bed. Everything neatly placed and positioned appeased Kayla, and the spaciousness topped the cake. From what she had seen on television, she assumed the room would look like a big closet stuffed with a bed, counter, and a separate area for a toilet and shower, but it was just as big as a hotel suite with a bonus ocean view.

"I see you got the hook up," Bryan said as he picked up the complementary champagne bottle lying in a bucket of ice.

"Oh, there's free champagne too? Wow!" Kayla added.

"Yeah, this is twice the size of a regular room. Someone must really favor you."

Kayla sensed a little sarcasm in his voice, but didn't want to jump to conclusions because it could have been his way of joking.

"You never told me you been on a cruise before."

"Probably because you never asked," he responded, sounding even more sarcastic.

"Okay, Bryan, I just figured you would have mentioned it at some point between now and you finding out we were going together." She was beginning to get annoyed.

"What? Was that some type of disqualification or something? I wasn't allowed to have previously come with anyone else?"

"What is your problem all of a sudden? You know what, just drop it because I am getting aggravated and we just got here."

"Oh my Gosh, do you really get pissed off that fast at a joke?"

"Just drop it, Bryan," she sighed, shook her head, and went into the bathroom to take more pills. Once she came out, Bryan was standing on their private deck with his arms folded. He slid open the door, motion for Kayla to come outside then wrapped his arms around her waist.

"I'm sorry, I've been stressed lately, but that doesn't mean I should be taking it out on this beautiful woman standing before me."

"It's fine, let's just go get some drinks and grab a bite to eat."

"Wait," he said as he ran over to the table and grabbed two glasses and the champagne, "not until we toast."

"What are we toasting to?" She asked.

He paused, gave her a seductive smile and said, "A delicious experience on this deck."

As they walked back to the main room entrance, Kayla again became enchanted by the crystal chandeliers and accents of contemporary neon lightning that flavored the ceiling trimmings. She remained in awe as a string quartet serenaded entering guest with a soft blend of moonlight sonata from Beethoven's symphony. Mentally drifting from her surroundings, she begun to wonder, *did she really see Jessica, and if so, was George there as well.* She knew a few years had passed, but this new investigation launched by Dana's mom had Kayla on the edge. She figured she was likely the only one who could link Dana with George. If the investigation was back in full swing, she knew the police would question her again very soon. At that moment, it dawned on Kayla that Dana had to have been almost full term in her pregnancy at the time of her death!

Perhaps Dana's mom was trying to round up suspects for a DNA match from the baby. Another overwhelming feeling came over her. Kayla had tried to suppress the situation for so long that she hadn't even thought about the fact that Dana may have delivered the baby before she died. It suddenly had begun to make sense in Kayla's mind. The reason Dana's mom held out on the investigation may have been out of fear that the person or people involved in the ridiculous alleged suicide would try to harm the baby too if they knew it was alive. Kayla had to know. She had begun to feel guilty. What if she didn't do all she could have done for Dana? What if giving Dana's mom George's name would bring peace to Dana's family and protect Dana's baby? On the other hand, what would happen to Jessica if she knew that her husband possibly fathered her cousin's child and murdered her? Better yet, who would protect Kayla and her son? Tears welled in her eyes as she pondered the lose-lose situation.

"Earth to Kayla," Bryan said as he waved his hand in her face.

"Oh, I'm sorry, baby, I got lost in my thoughts."

"I see. Let's go sit at the bar tables like we did on our first date," he said and smiled.

Kayla agreed as they sat down and immediately ordered two patron margaritas.

"What got you so distracted tonight?" He asked.

"What do you mean?"

"Your attention is obviously elsewhere right now, what's up?"

"Nothing baby, I'm just amazed that's all."

Kayla had already told Bryan about everything that went down in Atlanta, but as much as Kayla wanted to fill him in on her thoughts, she didn't want to be Debbie downer. Besides, she wasn't even sure if she had seen Jessica so why rock the boat. She just wanted to be closer to Bryan. She wanted him to touch her, hold her, and kiss her. She wanted to pretend they were acting out a scene in a love story.

"I was also thinking about how handsome you look in your Chaps and khakis."

"Really," he blushed, "you're lying, but I love it."

"What makes you think I'm lying? You are a very sexy man and I am lucky to have you in our lives."

He looked deep into her eyes as if he was trying to determine rather or not she meant it.

"What is it about me that make you feel so lucky?" He asked.

"You always make me feel like I am the most important person in the room no matter where we are. You care for Nicholas and I can tell you care for me a lot as well."

He looked down and shook his head. Kayla assumed he was guilty of something or something was wrong with what she said. Kayla went from being elated to concerned.

"Kayla," he started as he grabbed her hand and looked her in the eyes, "I'm sorry, but this time you're wrong."

"Wrong? A-About what?" She stammered.

"I love Nicholas and I am in love with you."

Kayla felt her heart skip a beat as she exhaled in relief. He got up, grabbed her hand, and escorted her to the dance floor. He held her tight as he whispered, "I promise I really do love you," in her ear.

After a night of dancing, mingling on the deck, and drinking with socialites, Kayla and Bryan headed back to their room. While staggering in the door from their intoxication, they laughed and joked about the night's festivities and people they met. She sat on the love seat and took off her shoes, then reclined on a pillow.

"I'm going to hop in the shower unless you wanted to first," he offered.

She waved for him to go ahead and turned on the television. About a half hour later, Bryan came out of the bathroom only to find Kayla sleeping peacefully on the couch. He turned off the television, lifted her up, and then carried her to bed. Kayla had on long sequenced styled blouse and tights, so he assumed she wouldn't sleep comfortably in the blouse. He raised her up and gently slid the shirt over her head then replaced it with one of his clean t-shirts. He rolled the pulled back covers over her body and softly kissed her on the forehead as he whispered, I love you.

The next morning, Kayla woke up with a headache and cramping in her stomach. Bryan wasn't in the bed when she turned over, so she got up and called his name while knocking on the bathroom door. *Did he seriously just leave me in here without a heads up or anything,* she thought? She grabbed her pills then went into the bathroom to take a shower.

She couldn't remember exactly what happened the night before, but she figured sex wasn't part of the equation, since she had on the same tights and panties and her kitty cat felt the same. As she stepped into the shower, she began to wonder why Bryan didn't wake her. They had been together almost six months now, so how could he be alone with her on a big romantic ship and not have sex on his mind? He had just told her he loved her, but as what, a sister? Kayla stood in the shower feeling hurt and puzzled as water ran against her face. Either Bryan wasn't as attracted to her as he claimed to be, or maybe he wasn't attracted to women at all. By the time she had gotten out the shower dripping wet with only a towel wrapped around her, Bryan was in the room watching television on the sofa.

"Good morning, beautiful. I brought you some fresh fruit. I figured it would hold you over until we went down to get some breakfast," he said as he quickly turned his attention from her back toward the television. Kayla couldn't contain her emotions. She was sexually frustrated and the pills seem to be having a diverse effect.

"Here I am, standing here butt naked with a towel wrapped around me and all you can think about is breakfast."

"Yeah, breakfast would be nice right about now," he calmly, but sarcastically stated not even looking her in her direction.

"So would a Fuck!" she screamed.

Bryan instantly turned off the television and gave her his undivided attention. He gave her a looked she had never seen him give her. She knew he was pissed, but it secretly turned her on.

He walked over and stood in front of her with his piercing eyes. She was hoping he would push her against a wall and screw her brains out. Instead, he gently laid both hands on her shoulders.

"I guess you're going to have to get use to guys who don't take advantage of drunken pussy."

"Let's get this straight, ding-dong; I wasn't drunk, I just happened to fall asleep after a long day of traveling and a few drinks. However, I can definitely tell you what I was and what I am, horny as hell with a man who acts like I am not attractive enough for him to make a move on," she raged as her voiced trembled.

His stare softened as he sat her down on the bed and kneeled down in front of her.

"Kayla, you are beautiful, hot, sexy, and everything in between. Honestly, most women I meet I hit on the first night or week of meeting them, and then a few weeks later I'm bored. I'm tired of that, it's old, so with you, I wanted to establish the feelings first, then make love. It seems like when I'm trying to do things the right way; I'm getting chastised for it."

"I guess." She softly replied.

"Believe me you, I'm guaranteed to give you exactly what you want in the best way. I would just like to take my time and develop something authentic."

"Well, I've never seen an attractive man go months without relieving himself. All men have to have some right?"

"First off, I'm not your average man and who said I didn't keep a bottle of lotion handy at all times," he joked.

After a slight giggle and giving him an "I don't believe you look" she shook her head in truce. Just as she was about to get up, he grabbed her from behind the legs, pulled her pelvic to his face, slowly began to tongue her clitoris under the towel. As much as she wanted to protest, since she felt he was only doing it because of her complaining, it was the most amazing oral sex she had ever received.

The way his mouth played swords with her clit was intense. He gently sucked her vagina enjoying the flavors of her body. The feeling was so amazing that her toes curled as the pressure from his slithering tongue shook her in pleasure. After he got up and went into the bathroom, she lied there shocked yet sexually relieved. She wondered *what is going on with Bryan. Is this his way of trying to prove her wrong, get her sprung, or cover up something else?* She wanted to ask him so many questions, but she didn't know where to start. He didn't seem abnormal about anything. After leaving the bathroom he came back and asked if she was ready to go. Deciding not to press the issue, she washed up, dressed, and allowed him to escort her to breakfast.

Chapter 12

Kayla had found a clean table near the exit area of the opened breakfast bar, which gave them an amazing view of the endless ocean. Kayla and Bryan had not said much to each other since they left the room. Although, it was an awesome sexual experience, the atmosphere seemed weird. Bryan was acting strange as if someone coerced him to do what he just did in the room. It was the most random, satisfying experience Kayla could remember having. Even, Bryan, himself seemed to enjoy the fact he had brought her great pleasure, but at the same time, there was some type of guilt or regret afterwards. He made her wish he hadn't done it to her. Something was brewing inside of Bryan's mind, but Kayla couldn't figure it out. Perhaps something happened earlier this morning that caused him to leave the room before she had woken up. Maybe whatever it was that was going on was causing the distance oppose to her, because he seemed perfectly fine the night before. With four more days left on the trip, Kayla knew she had to clear the awkward vibes in the air in order to enjoy the remainder of the vacation. She grabbed the booklet that was sitting in the middle of the table.

"So, what would you like to do today? We could go rock climbing, swimming, the casino, and oh, they have a pool party on the deck today?" Kayla mentioned as she looked at Bryan who seemed to be uninterested in anything she had to say.

"Let's do it all," he dryly replied.

"Bryan, I'm not sure what's going on here or why the cold shoulder all of a sudden, but I didn't ask you to do what you just did in the room?"

"What did I do?"

"Really? You don't remember going down on me like thirty minutes ago?"

He looked down and put his head in his hands. She must have missed his point or she completely misunderstood him all together.

"Look, Bryan, I'm not trying to be a pest, but you have been acting strange since you were missing when I woke up this morning. If you changed your mind about being with me, I can respect that, just tell me."

"Where were you when I told you I loved you?" He asked.

"Bryan, I heard you, I was listening but-"

"But, there are no buts, Kayla. I didn't tell you that because I enjoy hearing myself talk, I said that because I meant it. That's not something I tell women to make them feel good about themselves or to make myself look good."

"I know, Bryan, but you're making me come to crazy conclusions because you're not telling me what's really wrong. What are you holding back from me?"

Bryan didn't respond. He gave her a long deep stare as if he wanted her to see the answer in his eyes. She knew something was eating him up inside. A dark secret. Suddenly, Bryan's phone buzzed. He must have known who it was because he didn't even look down to check it. He continued to stare at Kayla ignoring the continuous buzzing of his phone. The longer he ignored it, the more aggravated Kayla got. She wondered, *who was he trying to avoid and why*? Whomever this relentless person was decided they were going to call until he answered. She knew it had to have been another woman. He picked up his phone, turned it off, and slammed it on the table.

"I got something I need to tell you," he started and paused.

"I'm listening," she anxiously responded.

"It's my ex-girlfriend. She found out I was seriously involved with someone and now she has been threatening to kill herself, call the police on me, and she said she's pregnant and wants abortion money."

"Pregnant!" Kayla exclaimed. She could feel her stomach getting sick. "So that's why we haven't been screwing because your still raw dogging your ex," she screamed.

"Kayla, please calm down and don't make a scene," he whispered as he leaned forward and attempted to put his hand on hers.

"Don't touch me," she challenged while standing up in combat mode.

"Kayla, listen dammit, I haven't touched that woman since I got with you. That is how I know she is lying.

If this woman was really five or six months pregnant, not only could she not get an abortion but I would have known by now."

Having a small bit of relief, Kayla stood there and gave his statement a thought. "So if you haven't seen her in all this time, why is she acting out all of a sudden?"

"Maybe, because the guy that she cheated with didn't work out or perhaps my mom told her, who knows," he suggested as he shrugged his shoulders.

"Okay, so why is it a problem for you to answer the phone and tell her she is done?" She asked as she finally gained composure and sat back down.

"Kayla, why do you think she is claiming to be pregnant?"

"What does that have to do with what I just asked you?"

"Listen baby, she wants attention that I am not willing to or care to give her. If I answer the phone, the type of person she is, she will feel its okay to call. I am trying to build a solid foundation and have a family unit with you and Nicholas. I am not willing to let anything or anyone come between that." He explained, gently stroking her hand. She crossed her arms and looked off from his gaze. She heard it all before. He stood up and asked for a hug while holding his arms out in anticipation of her embrace. She slowly stood up and obliged his advancement. Kayla did not feel like pressing the issue since he did open up to her, but she knew he was not telling the entire story. As much as she hated to deflect to childish ways, she had to know the truth. She had to find a way to look through his phone. She wanted to know how he was responding to the girl's text.

Later that night, Kayla and Bryan decided to go to the karaoke dance hall to have a few drinks and take the edge off. They chose to sit at a high top table at the end of the surrounding bar area that gave them a clear view of the karaoke contestants. They were making small talk, but the energy and vibe was at an all time low. Kayla had her mind on Bryan's authenticity and Bryan seemed to have mentally been everywhere else, but with them. He continued to text under the table and took a few extra bathroom trips, but she decided not to act upset and hide her curiosity as if she hadn't notice.

Her plan was to get him as drunk as possible so she would not have a problem being able to access his phone. She went out of her way to make sure she went to the opposite end of the bar to order drinks instead of him. Every round, she ordered two shots, one of tequila for him and the other a light lemon liquor to make it appear as if they were both taking tequila shots. After about six rounds and an hour and a half later, he became the life of the party. He had strangers buying him drinks, strangers buying them both drinks, and even a few servers were slipping him drinks when they assumed Kayla wasn't watching. Kayla didn't mind because even though he was intoxicated, he remained mindful and respectful of her, which was a quality that her ex boyfriends seemed to lack.

Kayla had quickly learned that a man willing to flirt in her face was definitely willing to cheat behind her back. Besides, in the process of trying to get him drunk, she got drunk as well. She had forgotten about her hidden agenda. She did not care about the argument, she did not care about his phone, and she just found herself having a great time with him.

An hour past midnight, they went back to their room feeling excited and energetic. They flirted with one another like they were high school sweethearts. Bryan turned on some music as he walked over to the double patio doors and motioned for Kayla to come dance with him. He gently grabbed her hand and wrapped his arms around her waist.

"You are so beautiful, Kayla."

"Thank you, Mr. Phillips."

"I meant it. You are everything I could want in a woman and I couldn't imagine myself being without you."

Kayla was speechless as they moved in rhythm of the tranquilizing melody; he softly kissed down her neck. Still dancing in sync, he slowly pushed her blouse off her right shoulder and proceeded to passionately kiss every inch of her skin as she closed her eyes in anticipation of the sweet seduction. Encouraged by the passion, she grabbed his chin to meet her lips with his as they wildly tongued during the removal of her leopard printed shirt, her fitted shorts, and last, the matching bra. He took a step back and admired her body.

He slowly rubbed the back of his middle finger in a continuous vertical path from the top of her breast, circling her nipples, then down to the beginning of her panty line where his vertical hold became a horizontal expedition inside her panties. He got on his knees and pulled down her lace underwear as he simultaneously caressed her wetness and then went in and out of her opening with his middle finger.

He kissed her on those lips then wiggled his tongue between her tight slit as her knees buckled from the sensation. She was in heat and she could no longer take the suspense. She dropped down where he had kneeled, pulled his unbuckled pants open, and locked her hands around his thick hard penis. He smirked at her satisfaction as he gently pulled her hand out of his briefs, so he could go and retrieve a blanket and condom.

After spreading the fleece blanket on the deck of the patio, Kayla watched Bryan as he pulled off his clothes as if he was auditioning for a Kevin Klein commercial. His lean muscular body looked edible as he placed the protection on his hardness. Sprawled out on the blanket, he sat down between her legs and began to massage her calves, her thighs, and then he focused all attention on the inner corner of her pelvic area. He placed gentle kisses from one side to the other, leaving her mid section aching for the attention. He was the king of tease and that turned her on more than any thing. She was amazed by his composure and his willingness to take his time while giving focus to pleasing her. He repositioned himself as he eased on top and slowly slid inside of her. Every kiss synchronized with his stroke. The deeper the strokes, the more intensified kissing.

His pumps packed power but were gentle enough to ignite the incredible sensation that began to brew in her vaginal walls only after about eight minutes into the sexual escapade. Everything seemed so unreal. She wanted to ask him was this the reason he waited so long to make love to her. He must have known that his sex game was on point. This was an ultimate experience she had never known until this day.

The tingling flow of sensation continued to magnify through her body. She began to moan progressively as he firmly grabbed her necked and whispered, "I love you". Seconds later, they both shook in climax.

Chapter 13

It was the final day of the trip and the last few nights on the boat were perfect. Kayla and Bryan partied, played, and had pleasurable sex several times throughout the day. Even the airplane ride on the way home was filled with intimate hand rubs and sudden romantic kisses from both Bryan and Kayla. They were in love and it felt wonderful. Bryan opened up more to her about how he grew up as a child and the fact that his dad left his mom when he was only six. He talked about it as general conversation with no emotional attachment, but she knew deep down inside it hurt and was a part of him that could only have restoration through his father, if at all, possible. She thought about reaching out to his mother to see if she had any information regarding where Bryan's dad may live or a even a relative's contact information, but it seemed as if Bryan and his mother were still on bad terms. Besides, she had not had the opportunity to be around Bryan's mom in order to see if she was approachable when it came to a subject of that matter. All she knew was that she loved him and was willing to go out of her way to make him happy.

Their arrival time for their flight home was a quarter after one on Friday afternoon. Exhausted and hungry after the trip, they decided to stop by Bryan's home first, grab a bite to eat, and take a small nap before heading to pick up Nicholas. Earlier on the flight, they decided to try alternating weekly stays at one another's home before moving in together on a permanent basis. It was still a big step since they hadn't been together quite a year, but they seemed to enjoy the idea of being domesticated.

Arriving in Bryan's parking lot, he told Kayla he loved her and gave her a quick kiss before opening the car door. Once he got out, he happily skipped over to Kayla's door in order to open it before she had a chance to. Suddenly startled by the sound of squeaking tires, Bryan flinched as policed cars swarmed them both. Kayla quickly got out of the car and looked at Bryan who looked just as horrified as she did. She instinctively threw her arms around him and held him tight.

"Don't worry, baby, it's just a misunderstanding. I'll be home in no time," he reassured as she felt his heart beat a thousand times per minute. Two officers ran behind Bryan, but they had to pry him from Kayla's grip. She screamed as they forced him against the car and cuffed him while reading him his rights. She sadly watched as they put him in the back of the squad car and slammed the door. Everything had happened so fast. Kayla was confused by how a perfect week could turn into a catastrophe. With her hands pressed firmly against both sides of her head, she closed her eyes wishing it were all a nightmare. She knew it was an empty wish.

Although the police didn't cuff her, they escorted her in a separate squad car and told her they needed her for questioning. Tears were rolling down her face. She was riding into the unknown, which kept her on the edge. *Is Bryan a drug dealer or something worse* she wondered. She then thought about what he had told her about his ex-girlfriend. A great feeling of anxiety had overcome her. *Why would a woman that he claimed he had no dealing with take this to a point so extreme?* Kayla's thoughts were exhausting her. Three failed relationships in one year were too much for her. She heard the two cops in the front making vague conversation, but she couldn't determine if they were talking about Bryan. Kayla couldn't wrap her mind around the fact that her world turned upside down within minutes. *Maybe I'm not praying enough* she thought. *This has to be God's way of showing me I'm not going in the direction he is leading me.* With her head against the window, she closed her eyes and began a silent prayer. *Lord, order my steps in your words. I've been going through one broken relationship after another and I'm tired. I've been searching for love, giving my love, and receiving nothing but regret and bitterness in return.* The tears began to roll again. *Why? Why can't I be loved and have someone who isn't about games or have dark secrets that only become known after the fact? I'm tired Lord. I need your guidance. I need your help. I'm walking in darkness. When I look in the mirror, I feel I'm lying to the person in front of me. I'm not happy and the pills hide my sadness. Help me Lord Jesus to find myself. In Jesus name I pray, Amen.*

Down at the precinct, they took Kayla in a dingy room that only had a table, two chairs, and a one-way mirror. It looked exactly like a seen from Law and Order. After twenty minutes, which felt like an hour, two different police officers entered the room. One was tall, Latino, and handsome with dark brown hair and eyes while the other was a short, stubby white guy with a balding head who walked in with his nose turned up. The Latino officer spoke first.

"My name is Officer Perez and this is Officer Kelly. You are...Kayla, right?" He questioned and smiled as he looked up from his notepad.

She nodded, his warm greeting slightly lifting her uneasiness.

"Well, you're obviously not under arrest because you haven't done anything that we are aware of, but we do need to ask you a few questions, okay?"

"Okay, officer with all due respect, I need to know what this is about before answering any questions."

"Ma'am, we will be asking the questions here," abruptly interrupted the bald cop.

"Officer Perez, since I'm not under arrest, I can go right?" She asked still staring at Perez.

"Yes, you can, but you do want to help out your friend, right?"

"Yes, but I refuse to answer any questions with the bald guy present," she boldly stated.

Officer Perez must have had more seniority because he motioned for Kelly to leave.

"This is absurd," he said, slamming the door as he left.

"Listen, Kayla," he began after making a quick notation on his notepad, "Bryan is in a lot of trouble and he is going to need someone who is strong by his side. I can't give you complete details, but he may be going away for a long time."

"For what?" She pleaded.

Officer Perez softly whispered, "Attempted murder."

"Is this some type of joke? That is impossible!" She protested.

"Calm down, Kayla, how is it impossible."

"We've been on a cruise for a week and even before that, he was with me, so there has to be some mistaken identity. Besides, Bryan doesn't even have the characteristics of a murderer."

"Well, have you been around a murderer to know one?"

"Look, Perez, I don't have time for smart comments from someone who claims their here to help me."

"I'm just trying to help and reason with you, Kayla, how long have you known him?"

"I've known him almost a year."

"Has he ever been violent?"

"No, he has always had the upmost respect for my son and me. He is not only a great boyfriend, but an excellent father figure as well. I honestly can't even recall him cursing too many times."

"Oh," he said as he cleared his throat and looked back down at his notepad, "did you know he has a criminal record?"

Kayla looked at him surprisingly, but didn't answer. She felt small.

"Look, Kayla, you seem like a good person caught up with the wrong guy. Go home, get you some rest, and call me if you need me, but my personal advice would be to stay clear of this guy." He slowly stood up, opened the door, and escorted her out.

Kayla was in disbelief. *Attempted murder and a criminal record* she thought! *I've been sleeping with a complete stranger.* By the time she made it to her car, she realized she had been down at the station for two hours. She was in no emotional position to pick up Nicholas, so she drove home, curled up on the couch, and close her eyes wishing it would all go away.

An hour later, still lying there trying to figure out what signs or hints did she miss with Bryan. She decided she couldn't take another minute of depressing and stressful thoughts. Brandy was always the one she confided in, besides, she really needed a fix to help relieve her mind of everything that was going down. She got in her car and drove towards Brandy's house wondering whether or not she should hang in there for Bryan or just give up before he caused further chaos in her life. Arriving in the driveway, she noticed that Brandy had company. After parking behind the black Charger, she reached in her purse and pulled out her phone. After a short moment of scuffling through her purse, she realized she had left it at home. She normally would call before showing up at someone's home, but she was in a crisis and needed someone to talk to immediately. Brandy would understand after she broke everything down to her.

She hopped out the car and accidently slammed the door trying to dodge a mud puddle next to Brandy's driveway. She bent down to make sure the mud didn't get on her shoes.

As soon as she stood up, she saw Brandy's front door open. *She must have heard the door slam,* she thought. Walking towards the door to greet Brandy, she saw a man standing in the doorway. She stopped beside his car in order to give them a little privacy, but she suddenly noticed the silhouette of a familiar frame, it was Quincy! Not noticing Kayla standing in her driveway, Brandy grabbed the back of Quincy's, Kayla's ex-boyfriend, neck and kissed him on the mouth.

"Oh my God, are you serious?" Kayla yelled.

Shocked by her presence, they both turned around in unison looking Kayla directly in her face. Giving no time for Kayla to respond, Brandy quickly grabbed Quincy's hand and pulled him back inside. Kayla ran to the door and banged as hard as she could.

"Brandy, are you fucking serious right now?" she yelled.

"You chose to associate yourself with this nobody ass bomb? Tell his bitch ass to come outside, I'm not pregnant anymore." Kayla was hysterical and ready to fight at all cost.

After about two more minutes of no response to her banging and demands, she got in her car and drove off. She was so distraught that she passed turns to her home and ended up going in circles. She couldn't think of any reasoning why all this was happening at the same time. *She fucked Quincy out of all people,* she thought, shaking her head. *That whore bag.* Brandy had her faults but this was Brandy at her low. Not only did she break the code of sleeping with her best friend's ex boyfriend, but also she broke the trust, love, and respect that Kayla had for her. Kayla began to sob. She just couldn't handle anymore-disappointing news.

A few weeks had passed and Kayla was in a heavy state of depression as she sat alone in the cafeteria on her lunch break. She hadn't heard anything from Bryan, Brandy hadn't called to even try to make amends, and to make matters worse, Dana's mom had began leaving her voicemails again, begging for information about a Mr. Goodbar. Kayla wasn't 100% sure who Mr. Goodbar was, she only assumed it was George because he was the only man Dana claimed to father her child. Then again, Dana wasn't the epitome of a saint either, so it could have been a different man. In fact, maybe George had nothing to do with her death. Maybe some other man was upset because he wasn't the father. Either way, as much as she hoped the case would get resolve, she wasn't a detective and she had too many problems to reopen what she wanted to remain a closed chapter. The only problem was that the messages that Dana's mom left were constant reminders of the fear she had for George as well as guilt reminders for not coming forward with what she did know.

When Kayla returned to her station, her head supervisor called her to the office room for a one on one meeting. She knew she was about to get wrote up for poor performance, but she didn't care. With her head down, she sat across from her boss and prepared herself for the lecture.

"I know this is a hard time for you. Here at Fairview, we not only take pride in our employees but we also care about the well-being of our employees and what happens to them. With that being said, we offer a paid week off for situations of this nature, but I personally would like you to take any additional time off you may need."

Kayla wasn't quite sure what she was referring to or how she should respond to her. How would her head supervisor know about anything personal that was going on in her life. People around the hospital were always nosey and Kayla was in no mood to volunteer information.

"I appreciate your offer, it's very kind and gracious of you, but I need all the paid hours I can get. It's only me holding down my household, so I'm really not financially stable enough to take an extended break."

"Kayla, you are so strong and determined, but if you carry all this weight on your shoulder, eventually your knees will buckle. You have a home to take care of, being a single mom, and then I know it has to be tough to have the role of someone being your patient and a family member to pass when things seemed so positive."

The bewildered look on Kayla's face made her supervisor realize that Kayla had no idea who or what she was referring to when she said someone passed.

"Oh my gosh, Kayla, you didn't know did you?"

"Know what?"

"Mr. Jen…Jenson," she stammered, "He died this morning."

"Of course, he didn't, I just heard he was doing fine the other day," she said in disbelief.

"Listen, I know it's hard to believe what has happened and I also know that no one wants to lose someone they care about, but you and I both know that all his pain and suffering is over."

"What do you mean pain and suffering?" She asked, holding back her tears. "He was just fine a few days ago."

"Kayla, I apologize that you may have gotten the wrong information, but Mr. Jenson was transported to a…Listen, dear, its okay. Take all the time you need off, alright?"

"Wait, wait, wait, this can't be right. Are you sure this is right, because the last time-"

"I'm sorry, Kayla, he's gone," she softly interrupted as a tear rolled down her face.

Chapter 14

Deciding to take her supervisor up on her offer, Kayla took her paid week off to reflect on all that was going on. As she sat alone in her room the following night, she knew she wouldn't be able to attend the funeral, but the least she figured she could do was call to give Raymond her condolences despite their last encounter. She knew Raymond had to have been devastated regardless of what his dad and his mom had recently been through. Jimmy Jenson was Raymond's hero. His dad kept him grounded. She shed a tear for Raymond at the thought of knowing that his dad would never get to see him get married or have children. Nervously, she picked up the phone and dialed his number. The phone rang once, but she quickly hung up. *What if he hates me* she thought? *What if I'm the last person he wants to hear from*? As reluctant as Kayla was, she felt that this was something that she had to do. She knew that this was beyond any situation the two of them had been through in their relationship. She picked up the phone and dialed again in hopes that the call would go to his voicemail, so that she could avoid the awkward conversation. However, the phone stopped ringing and someone picked up.

"Listen here, you little bitch," said the low threatening voice, "Don't you ever call this phone again for my son."

"Mrs. Jenson?" Kayla asked in shock.

"That's right, you think you can just be a whore and sleep around then call my son. You got another thing coming you dysfunctional piece of human waste. You and your little jail bird boyfriend are a waste of space."

"Mrs. Jenson, I know you think sleeping around with little boys make you seem younger, but aren't you a little too old to be taking cheap shots. I mean, you could be somebody's grandmother for goodness sakes."

"Put on your big girl pants, because I got a little news for you, Kayla. There will be no more of your bills paid at my expense. That will be the last little cruise you will ever take with Bryan, and oh, that bastard son of yours will remain fatherless since Bryan will be spending the next fifty years in prison. Ha, I win," she tormented before hanging up.

Kayla sat there staring at the phone. She couldn't figure out what was more confusing. The fact that Mrs. Jenson was more focused on her love life than her dead husband, or how in the hell did she know all those things about her relationship with Bryan. Bryan told her he hadn't worked for them in months, so what did she mean, "at her expense?" Furthermore, how did she suspect that Bryan would be spending life in prison? Bryan was clearly reaching out to someone, but it definitely wasn't her. As much as Kayla's mind told her to go her separate way, she couldn't hide the fact that her heart was stuck with Bryan.

A few days later, Kayla called the downtown precinct in order to get visiting hours for jailors. After getting dressed and dropping Nicholas off at preschool, she grabbed some breakfast and went to a few shopping outlets to waste time for the first set of visiting hours. After parking in the visitors' area, she looked in her mirror to make sure she had her face fixed to her liking. She walked in the precinct and informed the lifeless looking guard that she was there to see Bryan Phillips. She had begun to feel nervous once she walked into the visiting check-in room where all the other visitors were. After taking off her shoes and going through the whole security process, the guard handed her the sign in book for Bryan's page then turned towards the opposite side of the counter to call for his release. As soon as Kayla began to sign her name, she noticed Jennie Jenson's name twice on his sign in sheet. This really bothered Kayla. After about five minutes of waiting at the sign in desk, the guard came back and rudely informed Kayla that Bryan Phillips was released yesterday morning.

Kayla drove home feeling angry, resentful and saddened at the same time. She hadn't heard from Bryan in weeks, so how could he go an entire day after his release without trying to contact her. He said he loved her, but clearly, he didn't. No one puts someone they claimed to be in love with last. She should have been the first person he reached out to besides his mom. Kayla wanted answers and she wanted them now. She made a u-turn on a side street and drove towards Bryan's apartment. She wasn't sure whether or not, he was home, but somehow some way she was going to get her questions answered today.

Once she pulled up to Bryan's apartment complex, she noticed that his car was gone. Considering he was likely out on bail, she assumed he hadn't gone too far. She decided to wait until he returned home. She didn't want to chance him purposely avoiding her, so she moved her car a few spots down to the apartment building behind Bryan's building so she was out of his direct view. She positioned herself where she could see him and anyone who walked into his apartment entrance. She had a hopeful thought that maybe he needed a little time, but he was at her house waiting on her while she was waiting on him. Her logical thoughts knew that was too good to be true. It became even more evident when he pulled up twenty minutes later with someone else in the car.

Trying to hold her composure, Kayla's heart raced as she watched the passenger door open. She opened her door in attempt to be able to run up on him and whoever stepped out of the car, but she was startled when she saw a familiar face. Mrs. Jenson stepped out of his car in a shiny pair of silver and red heels with a short black dress looking poised in the presence of Bryan. Kayla examined Mrs. Jenson glancing around at her surroundings, giving the impression that she didn't want to be seen while pulling down the shades from the top of her head to mask her face. Kayla didn't know what to do as she sat there in awe with the car door still slightly opened. This wasn't the outcome she expected, but it was now clear why Mrs. Jenson was so upset the other night. Bryan had something extra going on with her, which meant he not only had been lying to Kayla throughout their relationship, but he had to have been the young guy that Mr. Jenson found out about so many months ago.

Kayla closed the door to her car and banged on the stirring wheel. "That liar!" she yelled, thinking of his indiscretions. She began to think about all the times that he acted suspicious and the times where he seemed like he was too good to be true. Mrs. Jenson was the reason he wasn't initially having sex with her. Mrs. Jenson was the reason they argued repeatedly on the trip, and she was the reason his black ass ended up in jail. These people were heartless and she was tired of being treated like gum on the bottom of a shoe. She got out the car and marched up to Bryan's door. She knocked so hard that she could feel the sting in her wrist. She heard a scuffle that sounded like someone was running or hiding then Bryan opened the door.

"Kayla, you can't be here right now," he forcefully whispered, obviously not expecting her.

"Like hell, I can't," she protested, while barging past Bryan's guard, "come on out Jennie Jenson, I know you're back there."

He quickly closed the door to keep the neighbors from getting involved by calling the police. Mrs. Jenson peeked around the corner to see who was causing the commotion. After seeing it was Kayla, she ran up the hall with her shoes off and attempted to attack her. Mrs. Jenson tried to grab Kayla's hair, but Kayla made a swift move by grabbing Mrs. Jenson arms and swinging her across the lazy boy chair and she ended up on the floor in the living room. Mrs. Jenson wildly kicked, connecting with Kayla's upper thigh as Bryan grabbed Kayla in her attempt to jump on Mrs. Jenson and wail on her face. With Kayla in his right arm, he told Mrs. Jenson to sit her ass down while he took care of the situation.

"Handle that, bitch!" Mrs. Jenson yelled as Bryan took Kayla outside and held the door shut so Mrs. Jenson couldn't get out.

"Are you serious, Bryan, this old adultery committing ass bitch," Kayla argued. Still holding on to Kayla with his other hand, Bryan pulled her face to his face and kissed her.

"Get away-"

"Kayla, listen baby, you have to believe in me," he whispered, now firmly holding her arm, "What I'm about to do is going to seem real strange, but just know that I love you with all my heart."

"What…What is wrong with you?" She confusingly asked.

"Listen to me," he loudly said as he began talking to the door, "I'm done with you and I don't want anything else to do with you. I'm sorry it didn't work out, but I'm in love with Jennie and there's nothing you could do to change that."

"Bryan, what's going on, are you serious right now?" Kayla said as she began to cry. Kayla thought he was actually going crazy.

"Have a nice life," he yelled, talking into the door again. He quickly kissed her again, whispered he loved her, and again said to believe in him before shutting the door in her face and locking it.

Still looking at the door, Kayla reached her hand towards the knob but didn't touch it. Instead, she slowly backed away utterly perplexed by what had just happened. She turned around and walked to her car feeling defeated as she began to feel the sting from the scratch left on her arm during the scuffle. She couldn't believe someone old enough to be her mother attacked her.

Even more hurtful, she couldn't believe that the man she loved locked her out while keeping her trifling ex-boyfriend's mother in with him.

Late that night, Kayla packed everything that belonged to Bryan and put it all in a bag. She threw in the pictures they took on the ship, the love notes he left on her dresser, and even the random gifts he bought her throughout the courtship. She erased all the text messages and calls in her phone in addition to all his contact information. She had to let go of anything that reminded her of him. It was enough that she was plagued by the thought that he would be touching and kissing Mrs. Jenson the way he did her, but the most sickening thought was the fact he hadn't had sex in months, which meant he was probably sexing Mrs. Jenson right then. Her thoughts killed her spirits, so she had to attempt to remove everything associated with Bryan. Her new motto was out of sight and out of mind.

*   *   *

A couple of months had pass, it was nearing the end of November, and Kayla and her immediate supervisor, Gabby, were making plans for her 25th birthday party that was also nearing soon. Although they didn't interact with one another on the cruise, they had gotten close during the absence of Brandy and Gabby was the one who helped Kayla through her deep depression. Although Kayla said that she wanted Bryan out of sight and out of mind, she constantly checked her phone in anticipation of a call that never happened.

In her weakest moment, she would call him only to be disappointed by no answer. She couldn't bare to tell Nicholas another man had left, so she told him Bryan had to go away to take care of his family.

She was so miserable that she strayed away from family, friends, her co-workers and lost several pounds from her severe appetite loss. Gabby was the only one who continued to feed her with positive thoughts and encouraged her to put faith in the fact that God would heal her heart. She told Kayla that she had to let go of the one thing that connected her to Bryan, which was her phone. She decided to change her number and to her advantage, this temporarily alleviated her Dana problem as well. Even though Kayla was on the road to emotional recovery, thoughts of Bryan still lingered. She figured one of the best ways to get over one man was to date another.

It was a cold Monday morning and Kayla prepared herself for the usual workweek. She dropped Nicholas off at preschool and drove to work feeling optimistic about her life. Once she got into the building, two men in black suits along with her head supervisor stopped her, showed their badges, and asked was she Kayla McQueen. Shaking inside, Kayla answered yes, as she looked at the frightening expression on her head supervisor face searching for answers. They immediately escorted her to an undercover car.

"Ms. McQueen, we had a small issue that has actually turned into something quite large. Do you know why you're here?"

"I'm…I'm not really sure." She nervously answered.

"You're not sure?" He asked sarcastically, "Your name has come up on several separate cases and you're not sure why you're here."

"No." She answered, deciding not to volunteer any information.

The two men looked at one another as if they couldn't understand why she wasn't taking the intervention seriously.

"Kayla," the other man softly spoke, "we are trying to get an understanding about what is going on. Your name came up on the Jenson case, the Walker case, and now the reopened Foster case."

"I have, at some point, been associated with individuals with those last names, but wouldn't know anything regarding their cases."

"You were picked up with the suspect in the Jenson case, you worked on the same team with Ms. Walker, and you were roommates with the deceased Dana Foster. What do you know?" The sterner detective drilled.

"I know exactly what you just told me." She answered.

"Kayla, you have one assault case pending and two possible murder cases being investigated. You're a link to all three of these cases. I need you to tell us anything that could help with the investigation," the pleasant detective pleaded.

Kayla wasn't concerned about Destiny or Bryan for the matter, but she did care about what had happened to Dana. She had been fighting that demon for so long and now she had the chance to speak the truth. Kayla knew how cops were and she was afraid that they would toss her name around to anyone she mentioned. She obviously wasn't under arrest, so if all else failed, she would have to get a lawyer if they continued to hound her.

"I don't have any information to give you and if you have any more questions, I suggest you contact my attorney. Are we done here?"

"Kayla, people are dead." The nicer detective implemented.

"I'm sorry to hear that, I mourn for their families, but I can't help you."

The detectives had no choice but to let her out of the car.

After watching them leave, Kayla went back into the hospital where Gabby and their head supervisor were standing around whispering at the front desk. Once they saw Kayla, they immediately parted ways as Gabby walked up to Kayla.

"Are you okay?" Gabby asked, touching Kayla's shoulder.

"Yeah, if it's okay, I was wondering if I could take a sick day. I'm not feeling well." Kayla responded.

"Yeah, sure...uh, let me okay it with Ms. Marshall. I'm sure that'll be fine."

Once Gabby came back with the approval from their supervisor, Kayla went to her car and cried. It seemed like every time things were going right, something else happened. Just as Kayla was about to back out of the parking lot, Gabby ran up to her window and told her to stop. Kayla was frightened by the horrified look on her face as she let down her window.

"I don't think you want to leave right now," she nervously said while twisting her fingers.

"Mr. Jenson's son just arrived in the emergency room."

Chapter 15

Kayla walked down to the emergency care unit to see if
Gabby was giving accurate information. Gabby had never seen
Raymond that she knew of, so she couldn't figure out how she
would know how Raymond looked. However, if it was Raymond,
she knew something serious was still going on with the Jensons. Mr.
Jenson was buried only a couple of months ago, then two detectives
came to her this morning about their possible murder case, and now
on the exact same day, Raymond was in the emergency room. She
was reluctant to go down and talk to him due to the earlier scare, but
she was drowning in curiosity. She wasn't sure how he would react
once he saw her, but if he didn't want to see her, she would say she
was just doing her job. She found the room and the holder that held
Raymond's chart information. She quickly glanced at the injury,
noticing it was similar to his dad's injury, a blow to the skull. She
opened the semi-cracked door and saw Raymond who was sitting on
the bed with his back turned from the door.

"I don't need anything, just my discharged papers," he fussed, still turned around facing the wall.

"Hello, Raymond." She cautiously said.

Raymond turned around and stared blankly as if he didn't know what to say. He turned back around and faced the wall.

"I was sent down here to check and see if you needed anything, so I'll be on my way," she said as she took a step back towards the door.

"Kayla, wait. Don't go."

"I know you're wondering how I got here. It's not really important due to the circumstances, but there is something I want to ask you that's important to me." He said, walking over to where she stood.

"Sure." She uneasily stated.

"My dad use to always tell me that you know a woman loves you when she doesn't turn her back even once for the hundreds of things you've done to hurt her."

"Your dad always had a way with words. He knew what to say and when to say it."

"That he did. You know, I asked my dad on a few occasions what did he think about me dating you, knowing you had a son. He said, 'son a man in doubt has already failed'. Even though he knew I wasn't ready, he always spoke highly of you."

"Wow, that's an honor to know, Raymond."

"I know a lot has happened between us lately, but it wouldn't hurt if we tried to start over." He said, grabbing her hand.

"Raymond, I-"

"Listen, Kayla, I know a lot has happened, my dad, your relationship with that boy, and my mom attacking you, but I still think it's a fighting chance."

Kayla stared at him. She couldn't believe what she had just heard. "Raymond, how did you know your mom attacked me?"

"What?"

"How did you know your mom attacked me?"

Raymond remained silent. He clearly had let his last statement slip.

"So…what I said about us got thrown by the wayside?"

"Us has everything to do with that incident. You found out she was sleeping with Bryan didn't you? Is this your way of trying to get back at Bryan?"

"I don't have time to talk about this, just think it over, okay?"

"Raymond, you are standing here with bandages wrapped around your bleeding head and you want me to think about a relationship?"

"Look, my problem is my problem and I'm not asking you to get involved." He argued.

"Raymond, if you're asking me to consider a relationship, you're not only involving me, but my son as well."

"Kayla that nonsense was the beginning of our problems. You were so focused on your son that you forgot you had a man."

"My son loves me unconditionally. My son doesn't leave when in doubt about mom's decisions. My son is dependent. Grown men can take care of themselves, so until you have a child, don't tell me how to take care of mine."

"Your right, Kayla, your son is dependent, which is the reason why he can't leave. Have a good life"

He stormed out of the room, walked to the front desk, and yelled for his release papers. The nurse calmly explained that the doctor would have to come to his room and go over his charts with him. Raymond sat down in the lobby as Kayla walked away after hearing the nurse tell him he had to go back to his room. There were a thousand thoughts running through her head as she walked back to her car. Only three people knew about the scuffle with Mrs. Jenson, so either Raymond found out and questioned his mom or his mom came clear and told him. Perhaps Mrs. Jenson had bruises from the scuffle, which prompted Raymond to question her. Maybe he saw her later that day with Bryan. Either way, it was clear why Raymond attempted a fake reconciliation. He wanted to get back at Bryan for not only stealing his ex-girlfriend, but his mom as well. With Raymond on a rampage, she hoped that he didn't also secretly blame Bryan for the events leading up to his dad's death.

Later that night around 9:45p.m, Kayla received a knocked at the door. Scared out of her mind, she ran to check on Nicholas, who was already in bed asleep, then closed his door shut. She went back into the front room to see whose car was outside. She really couldn't tell from her angle and the darkness, so she went to the door.

"Who is it," she asked through the door.

"It's me, Bryan."

"How do I know it's really Bryan?"

"Kayla, stop kidding around, it's me, I haven't seen you in months."

"No, I'm going to need to proof. Say something that only Bryan and I would know."

"Okay…The first time we made love was on the cruise we went on a few months back. I think, we danced to Tyrese, no wait, it was Tank. I slid the shirt off your shoulder, revealing your leopard bra and kissed you from your ear to your neck. I thought you were the most beautiful woman I ever laid eyes on."

Kayla opened the door as Bryan continued to explain in detail what happened. All the feelings she thought were suppressed came flooding back along with anger and resentment. Before she knew it, she slapped his face sideways. With his hands on his face, he grabbed both of her hands while looking her in the eyes.

"You know what, Kayla; maybe I deserve that because I know I've put you through a lot, but be careful before you hit someone because you never know how they may react."

"React to this!" she angrily said while jerking her hands away and attempting to close the door.

"Kayla, wait, I'm sorry baby," he pleaded as he caught the door, "Come here, please," he continued, wrapping his arms around the wailing woman. He held her tight as she effortlessly tried to move away. Bryan glanced at the clock, noticing it was almost 10p.m. "Baby, I know I have a lot of endless explaining to do, but I have something very important I have to show you," he claimed, leading her to the television and changing the channel.

"Bryan, listen-"

"Shh…give me just a second," he said, "I promise it will explain a lot about what's been going on."

(Music plays) Our top story today involves Jennie Jenson, owner and operator of First Dentistry, will be facing trial for possible charges in a murder case against her husband and victim, Jimmy Jenson, who passed away late August. No further details are released at this time. Jennie Jenson's bond is set at one million dollars. In other news tonight-

Bryan immediately turned off the television and looked at Kayla, hoping she would understand why everything happened from the broadcast. Kayla, still shocked by what she had heard, sat there still staring at the television.

"Now do you understand?"

"Understand what, Bryan that you slept around with Mrs. Jenson and who's clearly a trained killer."

"You don't get it do you, Kayla?"

"Look, Bryan, it took a long time to get over how you completely excluded me from your life and even before that, you left me in the dark, no wait, you cheated and then left in the dark. So, no, I don't get it and I refused to allow you to ruin my life again."

"Cheat on you? Ruin your life? Baby, I did this so we could have a life together."

"Let me get this straight. You were sleeping around with a married woman and used me to cover it up, but now that your little love interest is in shackles, you want to reconvene with me?"

"Is that really how dumb you think, or is that the anger talking?"

"It doesn't matter how or what I feel, Bryan, you abandon me. I gave my heart to you and you deceived both Nicholas and me."

"Now, Kayla, that's not fair, you know I care for my little man."

"Yeah, you cared, just not enough to stay with us, huh?"

"Kayla," he sighed, while kneeling down in front of her and grabbing her hand, "the first time I saw you in Raymond's backyard, my life changed. It was the first time I could remember being captivated by a woman. When Erica told me you were Raymond's woman, it didn't matter because I still watched your every move the entire night."

Clearly, you don't care about other peoples' women Bryan; you were already sleeping with a married woman she thought.

"And, in a way, I can't describe, the Lord showed me the opportunities I was missing." He continued.

"Bryan, I'm not trying to insult you, but you had to have known that you wouldn't prosper with a married woman in the first place."

"Judge ye not, for ye may be judged," he stated, getting up from his kneel and sitting beside her.

"Bryan, I'm not judging you. I'm just presenting you the facts."

"The facts," he laughed, "You wanted to know the facts. How about the fact I served time for beating my mom's ex-boyfriend until he was in a coma-like state because I walked in on him beating my mom until she was unconscious. How about I had to go on runs to drug dealers for my mom who got addicted to the prescription pain pills for the three surgeries she had to have to recover from in the hospital.

Here's something else you didn't probably know, I couldn't find a damn job because of my criminal record. My mom couldn't work and her disability was denied so guess what, Bryan sold dope and added a few more charges to the list. Long story short, I met Erica, who was my mom's physical therapist at the time, and that's how I started working for the Jensons."

"You met Erica, but ended up with Mrs. Jenson. How did that happen?"

He looked at Kayla as if she had slapped him in his face again. She could tell it was something he didn't want to discuss, but she had to know how deep his involvement was with her.

"Kayla, how is this going to help us move forward?"

"Honestly, Bryan, at this point, I'm not sure if there is a forward with us right now."

He sighed, "A month or so after working at the landscaping company, Mr. Jenson and I had gotten kind of close. He also use to tell me that Raymond didn't like the fact I spent so much time around Erica, but I knew Raymond was really hating on me because I was spending more time with his dad them him. Plus, Erica is gay, well bi-sexual."

"So you weren't into that?" Kayla asked.

"Sometimes its better to listen than speak. Anyway, Mr. Jenson asked me could I help him on a special renovation in his backyard. I declined at first, because I really didn't feel like doing the extra work, but he said he would pay me under the table and show me how to do big projects on my own.

One day after working on the renovation, Mrs. Jenson had brought us some drinks outside while we were taking a short break. I couldn't even tell she was his wife until he said something. She seemed over flirtatious with her husband, but I thought it might have just been me."

"How can a woman be over flirtatious with her husband?" She asked.

"Well, like she hadn't ever met me yet she was comfortable saying things to him like 'you know how I get down' and little odd stuff. I think he even noticed, but anyway, as the days went by, she would come outside with her hair styled differently and her clothes became more revealing each day. It seemed like after she saw me, she made it her duty to come fix us drinks or ask about our progress."

"Were you attracted to her?"

"Well…yeah. I am a man and she is a very attractive lady to be her age."

"Watch what you say." She warned.

"Listen, if you don't want the answer to a question. Don't ask from now on, okay?"

"Okay, you can proceed."

"I would say a couple of weeks of this charade went by until one day she called me from outside into the kitchen to help her bring out lunch for me and Mr. Jenson. Once in the kitchen, she began to ask me personal questions about why didn't have a girlfriend, my record, and my mom's situation.

Things that I knew only my mom would know, who probably told Erica in confidence. Mrs. Jenson then told me she knew people in high places who could help me with my record and my mom's disability. She gave me a time to meet her at the dentist office then said it was a date. I knew then she had other intentions, but I decided to play along to see if she could really at least get my mom her disability.

A few days later we met up at the office, no one was there, of course, but we still walked through the back door. As I was behind her while she was opening the back door, she rubbed her ass up against my manhood. She took me to the main office room then she sat on top of the desk as she laid down a folder. I stood by the door and watched her while she unbuttoned her white jacket, revealing the tight, dark blue dress she wore that showed her cleavage. She asked me what I was going to do to keep her happy or motivated, which ever it was. I walked over, rubbed my Johnson on her leg, and said renovate her life. I'm sure you don't want details of the rest."

There was complete silence in the room for a while. Although it hurt Kayla to hear about his explicit love affair, she partially understood the reasoning behind it all.

"Did you ever love her?"

"Kayla, I don't want to talk about this."

"It's best we get all of this out of the way now, so we don't have to review it in the future."

"If I loved her, I wouldn't be sitting here with you. I didn't have to tell you all of this and if I really wanted to be with her, you and I both know, I could."

"Bryan, the woman killed her husband to be with you, how were you going to be with her?"

"If it wasn't for me, they wouldn't have even found out she had something to do with it. This goes a lot deeper than what you think, Kayla."

"I need to know what I am dealing with, Bryan. How deep are you involved in this case?"

"That night after the party, Mrs. Jenson called me and told me she was in trouble and needed help. I told her I was with Erica, so I asked her what it was about. She said 'never mind' and made me promise I wouldn't tell Erica it was her that called."

"So you didn't see her anymore that night?"

"No, Erica called me the next morning and told me her dad fell down and hit his head on an end table, not knowing that Mrs. Jenson had already told me that her dad attacked her, so she hit him in the head with a vase in defense. She said that she didn't want the kids to know the truth."

"That's a lie," Kayla protested, "Raymond and I were both there when Mr. Jenson attacked her."

"What do you mean you were there?" he asked with concern.

"I was there when he attacked Mrs. Jenson, but I ran out once I saw Mr. Jenson throw Raymond across the room. Hours later, Raymond came to my house with fresh blood on his hands. Raymond claimed that Mr. Jenson had cut him with his keys after Raymond stopped him from running after Mrs. Jenson."

"I doubt that happened because Mrs. Jenson didn't say anything about leaving the house. She told me they got into it, but

Mr. Jenson still didn't know who the other lover was since it was hearsay from a source who claimed they saw two people entering the back of her dentist office after business hours. She said that Mr. Jenson left for a while, probably checked with his source, and then came back and told her don't let it happen again or he would kill her. At that point, she claimed that she told him she was leaving him and that's when he tried to strangle her or something."

"Raymond knew that his mom put his dad in the hospital."

"I'm sure he was there. He wouldn't leave his mom alone like that. That's probably how he got the blood on his hands, from helping her cover it up."

"Raymond may be lowdown, but he loved his dad."

"I didn't say he didn't love his dad, but I'm sure he wouldn't want his mom to go to prison and the way she was talking at first, she was going to pin everything on Raymond anyway, so her and I could be together," he said.

"Speaking of jail, Mrs. Jenson told me you were in for the next fifty years, why would she have been under that impression?"

"Well, it doesn't matter, because I'm not. I'm here with you."

"Bryan," she said a little louder, "why would she think that?"

"She tried to frame me, Kayla. Once I told her I loved you and was going to be with you, she tried to set me up. That's who was calling me on the cruise or any other time I was arguing."

"So you did cheat on me with her, didn't you?"

"No, Kayla. I will admit in the beginning I was still seeing her, but after I fell for you and got close to Nicholas, I cut her off."

"Hey, Mommy," Nicholas suddenly appeared, rubbing his eyes.

Slightly frighten, Kayla turned around to see Nicholas standing by the door in his pajamas.

"Bryan!" he yelled, finally waking up, running to him, and giving him a big hug.

"Hey, little man, I missed you so much."

"I missed you too, Bryan, I love you. Are you leaving again?"

"I love you too little man and I'm not going anywhere ever again, okay?"

"Okay, Bryan."

Later that night, Bryan and Kayla talked more about the things that had happened. They wanted to get it all out that night, so they could partially prepare for what the future may hold. Bryan told Kayla while he was in jail he had to come up with a plan to clear his name, so he begged Mrs. Jenson to come see him. During her visit, he said the right things to get her to post his bail and, of course, a week later, Mrs. Jenson sent Erica to get him. He also told Kayla he didn't contact her, because he didn't want Mrs. Jenson to find out about his plan. He had to make Kayla appear as a stalker, which was why he locked her outside of his apartment that day. He had to convince Mrs. Jenson that he made a mistake by choosing someone so young over someone more refined.

By convincing Mrs. Jenson he was in love with her, he was later able to set up cameras in his apartment and eventually get her to admit that she lied to the police. Although, he didn't get a clear confession on what happened after Mr. Jenson left the hospital, he did get Mrs. Jenson to admit where she hid the vase that she hit Mr. Jenson in the head with during the altercation and other incriminating evidence. Even though Kayla didn't like it, he also had evidence that they repeatedly slept together even after the death of Mr. Jenson and evidence of her confessing her love to him. They had several talks about them sleeping around behind Mr. Jenson's back. He admitted to Kayla that he didn't know a woman could be that heartless towards a man who seemed to be decent. Although, he wasn't opposed to it, he said the ordeal made him question the idea of marriage. As solid as Bryan's case sounded, they both knew they were up against a tough battle.

After seeing how Nicholas lit up after he saw Bryan during the night of their reunion, Kayla felt she had no choice but give him another chance. Besides, he did sound sincere about the entire ordeal and she was clearly still in love with him. On Kayla's birthday, Bryan had surprised her by proposing to her. They planned to see how a year of cohabitating worked then they would plan to marry soon after. She finally met his mom who was just as nice looking and down to earth as he was. His mother had been clean for a few months and she was getting her disability, which was less financial stress on them.

Even though, Bryan lost the contacts that Mr. Jenson gave him during his landscaping work, he was able to find a job for another landscaping company. His job came on time since he had to get a lawyer to fight Mrs. Jenson's claim that he was involved in a conspiracy. Kayla also mentioned her Foster and Walker situation to the lawyer just in case she needed him, too.

A month or so later, Bryan and Kayla found a new home in the suburbs of their town. It wasn't too far from the hospital and she was still about fifteen minutes away from her mom's home. For some strange reason, after she told Gabby that she and Bryan were engaged, Gabby started ignoring her calls and dodging her at work. Kayla was upset, but she was so used to being deceived by so-call friends it didn't matter. She still hadn't talked to her ex-best friend, Brandy, who had spread rumors around facebook that she was pregnant by Quincy. She decided that she wasn't going to let that or anything else was a non factor bother her. She had God, her son, her family, a man who adored her, and a whole life to live.

The Author

"Thank you for taking the time to read part II of Partially Broken Never Destroyed. I look forward to providing you with future entertainment that you will enjoy."

Feel free to also enjoy Part III, also available on Amazon.